A Friend of Humanity

A Friend of Humanity

Selected Short Stories

George Friel

Introduced by Gordon Jarvie

Polygon
EDINBURGH

©The Estate of George Friel 1992
Introduction © Gordon Jarvie 1992

This selection published by Polygon
22 George Square
Edinburgh

Set in Linotron Sabon by DSC Ltd
Cornwall, England and
printed and bound in Great Britain by
Redwood Press Ltd, Melksham, Wilts.

British Cataloguing In Publication Data

Friel, George
A friend of humanity: selected short stories.
I. Title II. Jarvie, Gordon
823.914 [FS]

ISBN 0 7486 6126 3

The Publisher acknowledges subsidy from the Scottish Arts Council
towards the publication of this volume.

CONTENTS

Acknowledgements

I am grateful to Fred Urquhart not only for the original suggestion of the need for this book, but also for early leads regarding the location of material. I found much background help in locating specific items in Iain Cameron's excellent M.Litt thesis 'George Friel: An Introduction to his Life and Work' (Edinburgh University 1987), which provides the reader of Friel with useful insights and facts, several of which I quote. Cameron's research benefits from personal interviews with members of Friel's family and with the author's good friend James Gillespie, transcripts of which are lodged with the National Library of Scotland. I must also thank Hugh Macpherson for practical assistance in the location of one particularly elusive story.

Finally, I am most grateful to Brian Elliot for permission to quote and use the author's copyright and unpublished material in this collection, and to the National Library of Scotland for access to relevant private papers and manuscript material lodged there.

Introduction

In his introduction to *Modern Scottish Short Stories* (Hamish Hamilton, 1978), Fred Urquhart says: 'The stories and novels of ... George Friel were admired by many people, but his work never achieved the wider acclaim it deserved. His short stories should be collected in one volume... '

As a long-time admirer of Friel's writing, I share this view. George Friel's published work was limited to a dozen stories mostly long out of print, and five novels of which two have come to be regarded as minor classics. The man himself is little known, a sort of B. Traven figure of modern Scottish fiction. In collecting his stories together for the first time, I wanted to make Friel's work more accessible and better known, and to throw a little more light on an elusive author.

This book is a *Selected Stories*. A *Complete Stories* is not possible, because Friel did not keep all his unpublished material. A *Collected Stories* would have had to include a further seven or eight unpublished items from the author's private papers in the National Library of Scotland, stories which—on the whole—seemed to me less successful than the stories published here, nor to greatly deepen my understanding of their author.

A word about the order of the stories in this collection. They are presented more or less chronologically, so that the author's development may be followed. There is not much doubt about the chronology of the published stories, but it is harder to date Friel's unpublished work. Like many authors, he tended to return to unpublished material, sometimes after long lapses of time, to revise or rejig it. For example, 'A Rainy Day' was submitted to magazines for publication in both 1934 and 1940 and rejected on both occasions. The version which appears here is the later one. 'It's a Wise Child' was another story which dated to the early 1930s in Friel's experience, but which was given a new twist or postscript with the passage of time and the experience of the war years. Thus the unpublished stories are slotted into the sequence only roughly. The following list is a summary.

PRE-WAR

'Helot'. Published in *The Adelphi*, December 1933.
'You Can See It For Yourself'. The first published story, which introduces the name, Plottel. Published in *New Stories*, February/March 1935.
'Her Brother Died'. Published in *New Stories*, February/March 1936.
'Home'. A Plottel story, published in *The Modern Scot*, January 1936.
'Thoughtless'. A Plottel story, published in *The Adelphi*, March 1936.
'Clothes'. A Plottel story, published in *Outlook*, May 1936.
'Brothers'. An unpublished Plottel story.
'Blackleg'. A Plottel story (marginally), published in *Outlook*, June 1936.
'Mr Plottel's Benefit Concert'. Unpublished.
'Onlookers'. Published in *Outlook*, August 1936.
'Unemployed'. Published in *Outlook*, December 1936.
'A Marriage'. Unpublished story.
'A Rainy Day'. Unpublished story.

'The Egg'. Unpublished story.
'Greater Love'. Unpublished story.
'It's a Wise Child'. Unpublished story.

POST- WAR

'An Angel in His House'. Published in *World Review*, April 1952.
'A Friend of Humanity'. Published in *World Review*, October 1952.
'Angela's Brother'. Unpublished story dated 1974.
'I'm Leaving You'. Published in *Scottish Short Stories* 1974.
'Quoth the Budgie'. Unpublished story submitted to BBC Scotland in 1974.
'A Couple of Old Bigots'. Published in *Chapman*, Autumn 1976.

Throughout his writing career, Friel suffered from a major professional problem—he was never remotely a vogue writer. In publishers' parlance, he was never commercial. As a result, Friel had the greatest trouble getting himself published at all. As an undergraduate poet in the early 1930s, he could get himself into print in the Glasgow University student magazine (which he edited for a time), and he managed to get 'Helot' published in *The Adelphi*, but his longer-term poetic enterprises were to founder on a rock of urbane indifference from publishers like Faber. Starting to get his short stories published in little magazines in 1935/6, he concentrated on that genre for a time. But here too it proved hard to get his work placed. No sooner did he find a satisfactory literary outlet for his work than it folded or was taken over or changed its policy. His big year with short stories was 1935/6—of the eleven stories he published in his lifetime, no less than eight date to this annus mirabilis. Thereafter the rejection slips far exceeded the acceptances. Yet Friel's 'Notes for Components of Short Stories', lodged with his papers in the National Library of Scotland, suggest he had fleshed out ideas for thirty or forty short stories, and one can only speculate on what little gems and cameos have been lost. Even with the novels to which he was finally to devote himself as a writer, Friel found it a full-time job merely getting himself published—four novels published in his lifetime, a fifth coming out shortly after his death in 1975, and no less than three full-length unpublished novels in his private papers.

Friel's inscription inside the copy of his novel *Grace and Miss Partridge* (published 1969) which he sent to a good friend succinctly summarises some of the frustrations he encountered getting his work into print:

IN EXPLANATION OF THE LONG DELAY

I wrote a story in 63
about a partridge in a bare tree.
I typed it clear in 64
and tried my publishers once more.
Back it came in 65—
Ah well, I said, I'll still survive.
It lay unread in 66
till Mrs Boyars, promising nix,
asked to see it again in 67,
accepted it—so all forgiven.
I got no proofs till 68
and that was November, rather late.
Printed at last in 69,
so now it's yours as well as mine.

(Quoted in Iain Cameron—see acknowledgements.)

In greater or lesser degree, Friel had this sort of problem with nearly all his writing. Only an author with the deepest integrity and commitment could have persisted in his literary labours in the face of such neglect. One cannot help feeling that it was a pity George Friel did not live a little later, or a little longer—long enough to participate in the Scottish literary renaissance of the 1980s with some of his younger successors—most notably Jim Kelman and Alasdair Gray. Today, one hopes, George Friel would find it easier to get a hearing.

So what kind of writer is George Friel? If we remember little else about the nineteenth-century American writer H D Thoreau, who came from the New England town of Concord, Massachusetts, we tend to recall his dictum: 'I have travelled much in Concord.' Paraphrasing Thoreau, we might say of George Friel that he had travelled much in Glasgow. Working-class Glasgow made George Friel, and neither his life (with the sole exception of the war years) nor his writing ever turned away from Glasgow. Friel wrote about the city because that was where he lived his life and that was what he knew. He was neither defiant nor apologetic about this.

What kind of vision of Glasgow does George Friel give the readers of his fiction? Well, he tries to give a picture that is *true*: true to the characters he created and to the world of working-class Glasgow. In a telling statement, one of his protagonists says: 'I've got the camera eye. I don't quarrel with anybody. Quarrelling is distasteful. I take pictures, artistic pictures.' (*The Bank of Time*, p. 184.) To some extent, this is also George Friel's credo. As his protagonist says, earlier in the same book, 'All great art is impersonal.' The artist merely 'selects the scene ... his vision makes it a picture ... the man with a camera is the artist of our time.' Or again, the artist creates 'the moment, the living moment eternalised in a photographic print ... like an ancient Greek frieze, like the maidens in Keats's urn.' (ibid. pages 94-5.)

How aware was Friel of the enormous risks he was taking by using working–class Glasgow for his fictional setting and then telling it 'like it is'? Who was going to publish him? What were the London–based publishing houses to make of social realism with a Glasgow background?

It is tempting to point out – as a parenthesis – that in his later, Bishopbriggs days, Friel was to live with the irony of one of the world's biggest book printing and publishing complexes on his very doorstep, with a flourishing fiction list, but with no place for his kind of work. Indeed Friel could bring Collins's factory right into the story called 'Angela's Brother'. The sights of William Collins – Glasgow-based publisher's but with fiction editors in London – were firmly fixed on the wider, cosmopolitan market, and their romances, war stories, detective stories, and 'light' fiction were highly-profitable market leaders. Social realism was not their forte. Nor was local talent, unless it fitted their markets – as, for example, did the (entirely different) later fiction of another Glasgow schoolmaster, Alistair MacLean. Thus, for reasons unrecorded but easily surmised, the Collins fiction editor in London was to reject two of the unpublished stories in this collection – 'Brothers' and 'Mr Plottel's Benefit Concert'.

In a rare press interview in 1972, Friel tried to defend himself against the charge that his subject matter was not very fashionable. Friel, deputy headmaster of a tough, inner city Glasgow primary school, said that he had no time for novels about adultery in the Bahamas or men with mistresses in Majorca and houses in London's stockbroker belt. 'In the life I know,' he said, 'a man doesn't have time for two wives, even if he could afford them.' As we said, To the accusation that his fictional world was rather bleak and depressing, he would reply that the world was like that for a lot of people. 'What am I going to do?' he asked. 'Put my head in the sand and say that everything is lovely? Surely a novelist, even in Glasgow, if he is writing about contemporary life, must tell the truth as he sees it. If I could see a lot of sweetness and light in Glasgow I would be happy to write about it : this is life. If you say what is going on then something might get done. But if you play Mr Glasgow and pretend that it's a fine warm-hearted city then you are kidding yourself, kidding the public, and pledging the future to no reform.' (Interview in the *Guardian*, 24 March 1972.)

But Friel is far more than just a naturalistic writer. There is abundant irony in his work, and not a little humour, even in his sombre moments. What on earth, for example, did the prattling Mrs Hamilton do or say at the end of 'Her Brother Died'? It is the reader's pleasure to surmise the depths of banality she plumbed. Equally ironic is the last paragraph of 'An Angel in His House'. Friel's irony is understated and unobtrusive, but it casts shafts of light across the general darkness of his fiction.

The author Elspeth Davie has tried to describe *why* one writes: 'out of the chaos of a short life we may feel the need to make something more or less whole and complete, to gather up visions and experiences ... so that they are not totally lost.' George Friel's short stories, like his longer fiction, bravely attempt precisely this. They are brave because they stick with and faithfully mirror the unfashionable world he grew up in and never left: because they offer no escape, or escapism.

The Pre-War Stories

How do Friel's stories relate to what we know about the life and experience of their author? The answer appears to be : to a considerable degree, especially perhaps the early stories.

He was born on 15˙ July 1910, the fourth of seven children of Jimmy and Sarah Friell, and raised in a room and kitchen tenement flat at 1172 Maryhill Road, Glasgow. Although the family's living quarters were cramped, it is not quite correct to picture the author's upbringing as taking place in a slum. The tenement community of the period was characterised not only by its liveliness and bustle but by its delicate social gradations and nuances, and it was quite possible for a large family to lead a 'respectable' life in such an environment.

George went to the local Catholic primary school, of St Charles, and thence to St Mungo's Academy, the first and only member of his family who went on to the University, which he entered in 1926. As an undergraduate he was active as editor of the student magazine, he was interested in left-wing politics, and he read voraciously in modern literature. His hero was James Joyce. At this period, George reverted to the correct spelling of his family name Friel: his father had changed the spelling to Friell because he thought it looked better that way. Characteristically, George wanted none of that.

It may have been the Glasgow University Magazine that triggered off Friel's creative writing. It was to be the only time in his life that he had any assurance of being published. He graduated MA in 1932, and proceeded to Jordanhill College of Education to prepare for teaching. From then until the War, George continued with his efforts to write short stories as and when he found time off from his teaching obligations. He worked as a supply teacher in a number of Glasgow schools until 1940.

Seven of the pre-war stories in this collection involve a family called Plottel, generally acknowledged to be based to a considerable extent on Friel's own family. The Plottels, like the Friells, were a large family, with seven children, living in a room and kitchen tenement flat in

Maryhill. Plottel Senior like Friell Senior was a failed insurance agent and occasional music-hall entertainer, unemployed for long periods. Both fathers seem to have been mercurial, indolent and irresponsible figures, not well-loved by their progeny, and unable to provide for their family's needs: 'thoughtless', as the terse title of one story has it. As a result, the Plottel and Friell families were matriarchies, with hard-working mothers assuming the key roles of breadwinners and anchors holding the factions together. It is a fair surmise that the 'helot' of the poem at the beginning of this book is George Friel's long-suffering mother. Or could she be Mrs Plottel? Further parallels between fictional Plottels and real-life Friells exist: notably the fact that both families are Catholic, and of Irish origin, and that the brothers Plottel like the brothers Friell tended to fall out.

An important atmospheric component of the Plottel stories and other pre-war stories is the impact of tenement living. The tenement neighbours are never far away from the action of the stories. They observe a great deal, however partially, and they provide a chorus of fates—or furies—commenting on the action. We have the 'gossiping matrons' in 'Her Brother Died'. We meet Mrs Houston, Mrs Higney, Mrs Reid and Mrs Farquhar in 'Blackleg'. And 'the matrons peeping behind their curtains' in 'Onlookers' raise the interesting possibility that this story and 'Blackleg' are in fact set in the same tenement, for the names of the onlookers are Mrs Houston, Mrs Higney, Mrs Farquhar, Mrs Plottel (in a purely choric role here), and Mrs Lennie. Mrs Hurley in 'A Marriage', and the men in the betting shop in 'Unemployed' all perform the same function.

An everyday fact of tenement life at the time was a high mortality rate, as we see in 'Her Brother Died' and in 'Onlookers'. Consumption was a common and often fatal illness right up to the 1950s.

An underlying theme of many pre-war stories, and later ones as well, is that of relations between the sexes. There is considerable domestic violence, either actual or threatened, most notably perhaps in 'Unemployed', 'A Rainy Day' and 'Angela's Brother', but not far from the surface in several other stories as well. There is no evidence that there was violence in the Friell household, any more than consumption, but domestic violence could be observed at any time. For working-class men, the worst insult was to be called 'Jessie' ('Unemployed' and 'Angela's Brother'). The protagonist of 'Unemployed' feels 'unsexed' when he empties a bin or washes a floor, because these activities are perceived by him to be women's work. This is a world peopled by men like Teresa Nolan's brother, who drink too much 'and batter their wives every Saturday night' ('Angela's Brother'). Friel infers no approval of this attitude: he reports it as he finds it.

Some Friel stories speak volumes about the social history of the period. Particularly fascinating cameos are 'Blackleg' and the story of the effects of strike-breaking on a Glasgow tram driver in the 1926 General Strike; 'Clothes' with its clear understanding of what it was like for a schoolkid from a poor home to be on the receiving end of free clothes from the local education authority (and stamped with the authority's initials: 'Why don't they stamp it on the backside of the pants too?' the boy asks rebelliously); 'Unemployed' with its horrific but unsensationalised description of domestic violence in unemployed Glasgow during the Depression; and the ironically titled 'Greater Love' with its glimpse of Glasgow in the Blitz.

Among the Friel archives in the National Library of Scotland, one of the most illuminating documents about this period of the author's life and his literary ambitions is the long-hand school jotter entitled 'Notes for

Components of Short Stories'. Here Friel jotted down notes and ideas for development as story material; here are pasted up newspaper cuttings that gave him the kernel of a storyline for his imagination to work on (notably the story 'Unemployed'); and here too he summarised his achievements with the short story during the years 1930-1937, with lists of story titles, themes, numbers of words, and whether published or not. Friel has written the marginal comment 'wholly true' against many stories ('A Marriage', 'Her Brother Died', 'Onlookers', 'Clothes', 'Thoughtless')—and occasionally refers to the source of the story, usually given as a neighbour. 'Home', according to the author's notebook, is a true story based on the experience of an aunt.

Also located here is a very telling literary comparison. Friel sets out a similar breakdown of the component stories of *Dubliners* by James Joyce (1914). Friel compares his own Glasgow stories of the 1930s with *Dubliners*, in length, organisation, and under a listing of 'headings to be covered' which included schoolchildren, students, lawyers, waitresses, domestic servants, street-walkers (amateur and professional), barmen, fathers, mothers, sons, husbands, wives, lovers and many more. It is clear from these notes that for a time George Friel entertained the hope of publishing a *Dubliners*-type collection of his own short stories of the 1930s.

These 'Notes for Components of Short Stories' with their Joycean references dovetail nicely with a reading of the vignette 'You Can See It For Yourself'. This most overtly Joycean of Friel's stories was also his very first commercially published story, appearing when he was twenty-five years old. The Joycean —type wordplay combined with Plottel's 'worldpleased' outlook and the sharp detail of his observation of the less articulate Anna Garshin and her mother force comparisons between Plottel and Stephen Dedalus.

The Joycean leitmotiv is evident elsewhere in the stories. See for example the references to Ulysses in the story 'It's a Wise Child', which has several parallels with 'You Can See It For Yourself'. And of course Friel's delight with wordplay is a feature of much of his later, longer fiction.

The War Stories and the War Period

George Friel married his wife Isobel Keenan in 1938, and they set up home at 25 Brackenbrae Road, Bishopbriggs, just north of Glasgow—this was to be their home for the rest of their lives. Friel forsook tenement-land for the comparative affluence of a bungalow in suburbia. Isobel was also a schoolteacher, and was to prove a supportive helpmeet of her partner's literary labours, helping him with early drafts and with typing. There were no children.

In October 1940, George joined the Royal Army Ordnance Corps as a warrant officer and was posted to England and, briefly, to Belgium and Germany. Isobel's family farmed near Annan, in Dumfriesshire, and she spent most of the war years there. It was to Annan that George came home on leave, as the Bishopbriggs house was rented out to the army till 1946.

The three, unpublished war stories all sketch in some of the moods and preoccupations of the period—notably the effects of the upheavals of war on long-term, stable relationships. 'It's a Wise Child', although listed here as a war story, really dates in the continuum of Friel's imagination and experience, to the period seventeen years earlier when he was an undergraduate at Glasgow University.

The Post-War Years

George and Isobel Friel returned to Bishopbriggs after the war, and to their previous routines. George went back to teaching, at St Mark's Junior School, in the Blackhill district of Glasgow, in October 1947, and remained there till 1960. From 1960 till 1973, he was assistant head teacher at St Philomena's Primary School, in Glasgow. In addition to his teaching, he was now trying to write full-length novels. The first attempts (*So I Was Told* and *No Other Herald*) were unsuccessful, in spite of several rewrites over a period of years. The big break came in 1959, when *The Bank of Time* was published by Hutchinson. Four other novels were to be published by John Calder: *The Boy Who Wanted Peace* (1964), *Grace and Miss Partridge* (1969), *Mr Alfred, M.A.* (1972) and *An Empty House* (1975). The last book came out in May 1975, two months after George's death from cancer (5 March 1975). In his later years, Friel tried his hand at radio and TV scriptwriting, and continued to turn out the occasional story. Ill health compelled his early retirement from teaching in 1973. Isobel Friel survived her husband till 1985.

The following poem, dated March 1974, is in George Friel's private papers lodged with the National library of Scotland. It is an interesting testimony – perhaps a little weary, perhaps a little defiant – of an accomplished story writer committed to a high and exacting standard of literary integrity. And it is perhaps an appropriate lead-in to the stories themselves.

ON AN UNPUBLISHED SHORT STORY

Seven times I wrote this story,
Not for cash or fame or glory,
Just to get the telling right
Though it never see the light
If it's printed I confess
Truly I could not care less.

Helot

SHE stood at the window twisting the ring on her finger,
tugging the curtain, then twisting her ring again....
the obvious rhyme is linger;
well, she lingered, she lingered there then:
tired as these words look tired,
resentful as they,
at the slow darkening of another Day.

The world was tired, trying to lean
its weight on words, and the words were tired too.
She saw what she had always seen,
an empty scene,
wearily answered *No* and yet admired too.

Words are tired things, resentful things:
that is why she never sings,
but rolls her necklace round her fingers,
life tied to a sequence as rhymes are tied.
So she lingers, knowing the rhyme is lingers,
standing at the window twisting her ring with tired
  fingers.

You Can See It For Yourself

Worldpleased with the foreclaimed wealth of examination fees and a few shillings balance in his pocket, he stood in shelter at seven o'clock, and easily conscious of the triumph of circumstances he was content she had nothing burdening her and nothing to burden him.

'I'm not going back,' she said at once.

'Not going back where?' he asked, staring at her in heart-quickened alarm defeatedly seeing the end of a brief calm. She gestured homeward.

'But I thought everything was all right,' he worded peevishly. 'I don't understand. You said everything was all right.'

She spoke in bewildering darts of circular explanation. The provocation and its repeated sordidness he gathered, and her lonely hate. Wordlessly he knew he should have expected it. Twice she had left her mother and twice returned, and then there seemed tranquillity. Now she saw there had been again the same scenes she had fled from before. Chatteringly she veiled her helpless misery, in nervous unbalance asserting her determination to stay away.

They moved by habit to mechanical entertainment, and came out to streets mottled under a sweeping wind. There she admitted she could do nothing. The dependence of her future was sharp to her again, and she submitted to return. Then knowing the wish still lurking in her defeat, seeing her bitterness that she could not do what she felt emotionally inevitable, he strove to distract her by questions of the cost of a room and of food, and how cheaply she could live alone until and after she began the work she expected. She spurned that futility, till doubtingly in his persistent queries she saw his meaning, and looked with wavering resolve at the note and coins he offered her.

Even if she failed with the job, she could live alone for a week with his money and have the victory of seven days self-sufficiency; it would keep her till she saw what she could best do, he argued. And while he persuaded her to the course he knew she wished and saw her re-risen determination gloss her future's paupered dependence, he wondered where, in his own poverty, he could borrow the examination fees he was giving her.

She stayed six weeks with friends, worsening in health and spirits. When he visited her she apologized with explanations.

'I couldn't get even a room anywhere else,' she said, 'for what I'm paying here and getting my food too. It's a change for the worse in one way. Mrs. Gomme buys the cheapest of everything. That's why the tea is so tasteless. My mother isn't like that. She believes in getting good food if she gets nothing else.'

Tired to see time's irony that now she praised her mother, veering with the folly and instability of it all, he advised her to go back. Her mother had written, pleading loneliness and heartbreak. She could return in victory then.

'You're not being fed here, you don't seem even to be getting proper sleep,' he said. 'If you stay here any longer you'll just fade away. You can't afford to stay in lodgings with fifteen shillings a week.'

'I'm not going back,' she declared. 'It would just be the

same old story—her lying drunk, shouting and quarrelling. I'm not going back, and that's all about it.'

Diffidently he persisted, then her stubbornness suddenly crumpled and she wept.

'You don't know the half of it!' she cried. 'You don't know—I can't go back.'

'What is it then?' he asked, old before her childlike weakness. 'If it's only that she's drunk once a week, go back. You're used to that. You make too much of it. I've heard her when she's drunk. She just chatters. Surely you can suffer that when you'll be properly fed and have some money for yourself. Your mother will dress you, your mother will keep you.'

'She'll dress me, she'll keep me,' the girl repeated impatiently. 'And where do you think she gets the money?'

'I know she isn't well off,' he admitted. 'But she has done it before.'

She straightened, wiping her eyes. 'I'm not saying she hasn't the money. I'm asking you where do you think she gets it. She hasn't a husband. And she has to live. Do you know what my mother is?'

In darkness as she wept again he struggled with sophistries. 'But she's your mother. It's her place to keep you. It has nothing to do with you how she manages that. She takes care of you all right. And you can't go on like this.'

'I'll go back then,' she answered slowly blinking. 'I'll go back, and we'll see how long it lasts.'

By the next week's end it was settled. 'I'm going back on Monday,' she told him. 'I give in. This is payday, and when I've paid all my debts I've three shillings left. I meant to go round again to her to-night, but I don't like going empty-handed: she hadn't a penny in the house when I saw her. And I need the little I have. Still, she's so lonely, I wish we could go round and take something with us and play cards with her—she likes playing cards ... make a good start....'

'I see,' he said. 'A pleasant evening by the old fireside. Well, we'll try it. I've three shillings too.'

'Listen then,' she hurried. Watchfully he guided her clear of a mumbling and reeling drunk. 'I know what we'll do. A shilling for cakes and things for tea. Then another shilling for cigarettes—mother likes a cigarette occasionally. And—well, I'll put in my three shillings too, and we'll take her a drink. A gill of the best, two and nine, and two strong ales, one and twopence. Leaves us with a penny.'

'And what do you do about next week?' he asked slowly, unsympathetic with her extravagance.

She laughed, holding out her hand. 'Never mind next week. This is to be a celebration.'

Mrs. Garshin jerked her head in surprise when she opened the door, then effusively ushered them. She was well-made, fresh-faced and easy moving, about thirty-six. 'Oh, what a lovely fire, mother!' cried the girl, entering the old kitchen, taking off her hat and coat, strangely at home again. 'We'll have the kettle boiling in no time.'

She set the table with swift familiarity and dallied at arranging her shillingsworth of cakes. Uneasily Plottel listened to her mother's chatter. 'You're welcome here any time. It's you I have to thank. She says it was you told her to be sensible. She was round here on Thursday, and I never seen her look such a sight. Good lord, girl, says I, are those the only clothes you have? And the colour of her! Can't you take care of yourself like me? I says. Look at me. Would you know I was nearly twice her age? That's what comes of knowing how to look after yourself. My life would kill her. She sat in that armchair in the room, you know the chair I mean, one of the few things I managed to save when I lost my big house in Buccleuch street; those were the days when I had a house, with seven rooms and a maid, and she began to cry and she says Mother, that woman has me near starved. Oh, I know that Mrs. Gomme, never out of debt, the old slattern! My girl's few shillings were a godsend to her. And what did she give her for them but the leavings of the others? What was a bed? I'd give a bed myself to any girl that was on the rocks, and for nothing too. But I'd never shelter a girl that had a home to go to and a good mother waiting her.'

'No,' said Plottel.

'And I have been a good mother to that girl. There's nobody can deny it. I was only a girl myself when she was born, and I brought her up and gave her the best of everything. I worked for her, I slaved for her, and you see how she treats me. I could have put her into a home, couldn't I? But, no, not me! I love my girl too much for that.'

'Yes,' said Plottel.

'There's nobody loves her like her mother, if she only knew it. But she's flighty. She has run away before this, for no reason at all. She doesn't need to run away again. Let her settle down here and behave herself. I do everything a mother can.'

Turning from the aluminium teapot the girl said, 'We've something for you, mother.'

Plottel awkwardly brought out the bottles.

'Oh!' cried Mrs. Garshin. 'This is ... but not for me, thanks, not for me!'

'Don't be silly, mother,' said Anna. 'We bought them specially for you. After tea, then.'

'Ach, there's no harm in a drink now and again,' said the woman. They sat down at table nervously together. The girl held out the cakeplate, smiling and affectionate. Genuinely affectionate, thought Plottel: there was the bond of blood and a common past between them.

'These are lovely, mother,' she said, 'and you....'

She stopped. The motherward smile in her eyes became

a hostile state of fear. Someone was knocking at the door, quietly, familiarly. Mrs. Garshin was startled and flushed; touching her hair headbowed she left them. They heard her movement at the front door, her low response to a man's parched voice, then footsteps to the bedroom at the rear. Plottel looked obliquely at the girl. She snatched a handkerchief from her sleeve, shouldering his regard. The heedless movement knocked her cup over.

'I told you so!' she cried, covering her eyes, her shoulders drawn in. Then before her sobs made her inarticulate in another failure she spoke again. 'You can see it for yourself.' He saw the stupid-looking cakes sodden in a pool of spilt tea, the stolid bottles on a sidetable, and regretted the money wasted.

Her Brother Died

Mr Ramsey, a clerk in the offices of a Clydebank engineering firm, went to church every Sunday in a suit he wore only on that day, with a large Bible under one arm and his wife on the other. Behind them their two children, a boy and a girl, walked demurely. The mother was a small, dreamy woman, anæmic-looking, and the children were thin, with large, staring eyes.

When her husband died unexpectedly, Mrs Ramsay looked dreamier than ever, and stopped going to church. Freed from the strict supervision of their father, the boy and girl played in the backyard, where in his lifetime they had been forbidden to go because he was sure they would learn nothing good from the children there, so badly brought up that they swore, pilfered and fought, and were never taken to church. The girl was always at her brother's heels then. He was two years older than she was, and she relied on him in everything. But he was a timid leader, and when he first began to go into the yard the other children called him 'Jessie' because his sister was always with him, and jeered at his cowardice and thinness. So the boy and girl wandered round the yards, hovering silently together on the fringe of the noisy games and squabbles of the others.

After a while, the boy was allowed to enter a game occasionally, and his sister remained outside, watching him with large, docile eyes. When the game allowed it, he secured her a place in it beside the sisters of the other boys; but she had always to be on his side, or she was clumsy and nervous, ready to burst into tears if any of the children callously mocked her.

One evening in spring, when she was thirteen and grown into a shy big girl, she dallied in the backcourt with her brother after a crowded, quarrelsome game had broken up. As they played alone at ball-throwing, another boy and girl came into the yard, both between fourteen and fifteen; and seeing them, her brother leaned against the wall, as if ashamed to be seen playing in the yard at his age with his sister, disowning her and the game. But he livened to it again when the others merrily seized the ball and began to play.

The yard grew dark in the late twilight as they played on, and seeing them take possession of the ball as if it were theirs, cutting her out, the girl wanted to ask her brother to go upstairs with her, but she was afraid to open her mouth. Standing unnoticed, nervously twisting her fingers, she hated the elder girl for her restless impudence, her loud voice and her gay manner, and jealously watched her domineer the two boys.

Then their haphazard game died away, and her brother returned to her side as, whispering and laughing, the other two scuffled into the corner of the yard and wrestled against the broken paling. She wanted to go away, and glanced in confusion at her brother; but he was staring at the boy and girl embraced in the corner, his mouth hanging open in a foolish grin. Then with a mighty heave the girl pushed the boy away, and in a voice bright with boldness said: 'Try it with Mona Ramsay!'

She looked in alarm from one to the other, blushing self-consciously, when she heard her name mentioned; and turning again to her brother for support in her vague terror, she saw him move awkwardly over to the girl lolling alone in the corner, his arms reaching uncertainly forward. Hurt and humiliated at his leaving her and ashamed to see him try to embrace the laughing girl flaunting her skirts at him, she was so upset she did not see the other boy come at her side. Then suddenly she felt his arm around her, and before she could move he kissed her clumsily.

When he let her go, she ran in a panic over to the closeway out of the yard, her lower lip trembling, her face scarlet. Then she stopped there, expecting her brother to come loyally forward. But he was still in the corner, his back turned to her, and the girl was clenching his hand and so twisting his fingers that he was bent in pain, squirming to release himself. Standing alone, in an agony of confusion, she saw the other two stare at her in amusement. Her lower lip increased its trembling, and in a moment she was sobbing. Jerking round, her hand at her eyes, she ran through the close, and for the first time went upstairs alone. When her brother came in, she did not speak to him.

But from that night she began to change. She stopped depending on her brother, and jeered at him as often as she could find the slightest opportunity. His excited attempt to kiss Sadie Cameron, and the easy way that girl had twisted his fingers and kept him harmlessly off, made her look down on him. She sought to imitate that girl, joined her to be chased by boys, and remained with her in the backyard late when the children who were still at school had gone upstairs. No longer timid and silent, she delighted in teasing the youths who came near her, and found an exciting power in her new boldness. She saw she could make them as flustered and clumsy as her brother had been, and that pleased her.

When she left school and became too old to play in the yard, she went her own way at night, parading the streets till eleven o'clock with a chosen ally, walking from the

Barracks to the Cross and back again, courting the approach of strange boys and then standing lingeringly with them in closeways and shop-entrances. Her big eyes gave her face a doll-like look, and she was fond of posing in front of a mirror, fingering her face and appraising it, using rouge and powder with extravagance before she was a year left school.

Between sixteen and seventeen she began to frequent dance-halls. Unruled by her feckless mother, she kept the greater part of her wages as an office girl to herself, and every week she had some new trifle to deck out her dress. She became notorious for her style, not content to be merely smart, but seeking always something outstanding, some frill or hue that would distinguish her from everybody. The gossiping matrons compared her unfavourably with Ella Vernon, who was always fashionable and yet always quiet, and righteously asked each other what the mother was thinking of, to let the girl go dancing every night in the week and be dolled up like that on the few shillings she would get in an office. They felt their dark hints and worst suspicions fully justified when, on a new film star making blond hair the symbol of passionate beauty, the girl who until then had been a dull brunette appeared proudly hatless. Her hair was a light yellow, nearly white. The unnatural splendour of it, waved and brilliant, made the neighbours sure she was on the downward path.

And all this time she was becoming more and more alien to her brother. Her behaviour shocked him, but he was afraid to speak to her. His two years seniority seemed negligible now they were both beginning to be grown up, and he felt he had no authority over her; sometimes, with a vague recollection of her childhood dependence on him, he wondered how it had come to pass that now she bossed him and lived so wilfully different from him. He worked as a clerk in a factor's office, wore his bowler hat even after office hours, and was beginning to go back to the Presbyterian church his father had attended. Pale-faced, round-shouldered and spectacled since seventeen, he was highly thought of by the gossiping matrons as a serious, steady young man, surely a help and a blessing to his mother compared with the gadabout, painted girl.

But there was an element of sympathy in the praise of the matrons, for it was rumoured that he was consumptive, and the local historians reminded the younger gossips that the father had died from consumption. It was then in pleasure and pride at having foretold it, rather than in pity at his state, that they saw him in such ill-health that he was able to attend his work only irregularly, and finally, when he was twenty-two, become so bad that he stopped working altogether and lay all day on a couch by the front-room window, looking down on the main road leading out of the city to the land of the lochs.

During his decline, his sister passed from the local dancehalls, and —becoming more and more uppish and affected in dress and voice—went to expensive resorts, often with an escort who had a two-seater car. Added to the pleasure-hunting heedlessness in his sister, isolating him completely in his illness, was an increasing uselessness in his mother. The neighbours whispered she was already in her dotage, and to help her in her double task of housework and looking after an invalid, one of the childless married women of the tenement began to go about the house. It was not purely from kindliness that she did so: she was inquisitive, with little to do in her own house, and in her boredom sought the material of gossip. Also, she had a hankering to be rude to the daughter, to constrain and rule her as she was sure she could have done with any child of her own. But the wandered mother saw only that the gratuitous interference left her undisturbed in her sorrowful weariness and took out of her hands tasks she could never have finished without getting into a muddle. So two or three times a day she would say to the bustling, meddlesome neighbour: 'I don't know what I'd do without you, Mrs. Hamilton.'

After a long illness, the young man died at three o'clock in a May morning, and Mrs. Hamilton took brusque control. It was a situation perfectly suited to her talents. She pulled down the blinds, sent for the undertaker, arranged for the burial, organized a subscription among the neighbours to buy flowers for the coffin, and saw to the insurance money. Looking blank, and quite helpless in her grief, the mother did not even know what was being done. She clung to her daughter and wept in brief but frequent spasms, little trickles of tears running down her vacuous face, while her trembling hand tightly held a small handkerchief which she could not even raise to her eyes. And supporting her mother in their loss, the girl suddenly broke down and wailed for half an hour. But, after that she was dry-eyed again, and simply looked absent-minded. Yet her evidence of sorrow softened Mrs. Hamilton's hostility, and it was retailed immediately to the gossip-hungry neighbours. They interpreted it magnanimously, heads sympathetically nodding, as proof that the girl was not really bad at heart, but just flighty and empty-headed. And the eldest of them, looking back into the past with an expression of pathos at the transience of youth and human affection, recalled that the boy and girl had been inseparable as children. Then there was elaborated the tale of a sisterly love, deep, constant, and hidden, and every one was sorry for the girl who had suffered the great loss of her only brother, the only one she ever cared for. The mother, it was said, fortunately didn't realize what had happened.

Mrs. Hamilton arranged the funeral for three o'clock the next afternoon, and lived in the Ramsays' house till then, attending to the prostrate mother and the mute girl.

She tidied the kitchen in the morning, had the coffin with the body laid out in the front-room, and set out an abundance of wreaths and bouquets there, beaming with pride at the success of her subscription list.

Early in the afternoon she sat in the kitchen talking to the mother, trying, as she said later, to distract the poor woman. Wearing a black dress, her face pale and washed-out looking, the girl sat away from them with her elbow on her knee and her head on her hand. Then she rose quietly and went through to the front-room where the coffin and all the flowers were. The only sound in the darkened house was Mrs. Hamilton's prattling. Occasionally she stopped talking, hoping in her tender sympathy to hear the girl weeping in the next room. But when she stopped talking the whole world seemed silent. Then as it came near the hour when the neighbours going with the carriages should come in, she rose and went through the lobby, moving with reverent quietness, to fetch the girl to the kitchen in readiness to receive the visitors. The door of the front-room was closed, and with self-conscious tact she softly opened it and peeped in sympathetically. Her head jerked convulsively in astonishment, and her hand tightened on the door-knob to support her as she craned incredulously forward.

The room was dim in the twilight caused by the drawn blinds, and on the table in the centre of it lay the lidded coffin. But there were no flowers on it or round it or near it. In front of the wardrobe mirror, her black dress changed for a long-skirted, turquoise-blue dance frock that showed up her bosom and hips, the girl swayed and pirouetted and posed. One of the wreaths was round her neck, a single red flower was in her glaring blond hair, and in each hand she held a large bouquet. Other wreaths and bouquets were strewn symmetrically on the carpet at her feet, and when she swayed with her back to the large mirror, her arms slowly flapping, she looked thoughtfully

over her shoulder, studying her pose. Then pirouetting
again, bending her torso back, she tried another one,
obliquely appraising herself garlanded, picking out a
languid waltz between the scattered flowers on the floor.

Home

On a chilly morning in early spring, wakened by the alarm going off at six o'clock, Mrs Plottel eased away from the child who slept beside her and sighed resignedly. When she made the bed at night it seemed a wretched thing, with two old coats taking the place of a quilt; but every morning, long warmed by her body and the bodies of the two girls who slept with her, the makeshift bedding wheedled into a yielding comfort under their weight, it seemed the best bed in the world, the single shabby blanket and the two ragged coats unoffending in the darkness wherein only their warmth was known. So now she sighed, and her movement and the sound of the alarum made the other sleepers turn over muttering. With a scowl at their huddled backs, unsympathetic at their sleepy complaints, she slowly rose and stopped the shrill ringing. It merely disturbed them for a moment or two, and gave them the added luxury of lying there warmly conscious they had not to rise yet; for her alone was it the end of sleep, and she sighed again as she looked round the sombre kitchen for her clothes, trembling in the cold, her bare feet on patternless waxcloth.

As she dressed, she thought of the work before her and of her children and her husband. It was five years since Mr Plottel had last done any regular work, and his untroubled vanity amid their increasing poverty so irritated her that the house was the scene of an endless civil war, and the seven children, all still at school, were encouraged by her in their belittling of their father. The money he was given by the parish authorities was hardly enough to feed the large family, although if he came in to find there was no hot water immediately ready for his tea he would rant at the children that he wasn't keeping them in the lap of luxury for nothing, and they would have to smarten their ways or something would happen to them. The empty darkness of the threat had long ceased to frighten the children, and they would retail it with contemptuous mimicry to their mother when she came back late in the evening from cleaning the villas of the well-to-do out in the suburbs.

Today she was due to begin the spring-cleaning of Mrs Cowan's seven-roomed house in Muirend, and, looking for her shoes, she thought over what was in front of her. After five minutes of looking under the chairs and the bed, striking matches in the weakening darkness, she remembered she had taken them off in the front room, and when she went through there for them the sound of her husband's deep and contented snoring, the sight of him sprawling comfortably over the bed so that the boy who slept beside him was crushed into a corner, and the thought that she was going out to work while he would sleep there till eleven o'clock, so provoked her bitterness that she wanted to waken him. When she found her shoes, she dropped them noisily on the bare, wooden floor, and looked malevolently over at her husband's bed. But he kept on snoring in a slow, oblivious rhythm.

The sole of one of her shoes was cracked, and the other one was so thin that she could have forced her finger through it. Perhaps, she thought, among the odds and ends often given her at the end of a thorough cleaning, there would be some pairs of shoes this time. Returning to the kitchen, taking her coat from its peg in the lobby on her way, she saw the eldest girl lying with her eyes wide open.

'What'll I do about breakfast?' asked the girl.

'There's the better part of a loaf in the press,' said Mrs Plottel. 'And there's plenty of dripping. You can fry some bread.'

'And what about him?' asked the girl. Like a primitive tribe confronted with an evil spirit whom it was fatal to name, the children never named their father. If they departed from the simple pronoun, they used scornfully pompous titles: 'Alexander the Great,' 'Frankenstein,' 'His Majesty,' and sometimes even 'God Almighty.'

'Oh, there's an egg there,' said Mrs Plottel. 'It's neither good nor middling. But it'll do him. And he's well off at that.'

And indeed, in spite of their hostility, the mother and her children always surrendered to Mr Plottel anything there was in the house beyond bread and margarine. He looked at his plate with such theatrical amazement, courting attention and apologies, if he were given nothing but bread and margarine; he turned over the slices with such plaintive bewilderment, and even sometimes dared ask, with heavy sarcasm, 'What's this supposed to be?', that they were glad to let him have all to himself whatever extra there was, for the sake of a quiet life.

'And when will you be back?' asked the girl.

'About seven or eight,' said Mrs Plottel. 'Have the kettle on the boil. I'll bring something in with me.'

'Oh, you get paid today?' cried the child joyfully.

'Well, I expect so,' said Mrs Plottel grimly. 'She always pays me on a Wednesday.'

The other girl, wakened by the voices, stretched herself happily and said: 'Bring in fish and chips. And pickles.'

'And what'll I do about dinner?' asked the elder girl.

'Oh, do what you can,' said Mrs Plottel, irritated at the insistence on the eternal problem she would have preferred to evade. 'You'll get your tea when I come in. See if Peggy in the fruit-shop will give you half a dozen bananas till the evening. You can spread them on a piece if you get them,and that will keep you going till I get back. I can't leave you anything. I've only fourpence for my bus.'

When she got out to the dark, deserted road between the sleeping tenements it was raining lightly on a piercing east wind. Shivering, she regretted her bed, and felt her legs and arms stiff from the aftermath of the previous day's charring for Mrs Hutchison in Bearsden. She had borrowed the seven shillings due for that job before she did it, and now she hadn't even the recompense of money in her purse, but only a clinging weariness. Plodding to the bus stop, she felt the rain-sodden pavement soak its dampness through the broken soles of her shoes, and her feet were frozen.

It was just after seven o'clock when she left the bus at Muirend and reached Mrs Cowan's villa. Sleepy-eyed and unwashed, the maid let her in and yawned. The house was cold and dim.

'You'd better start on the sitting-room first,' said the maid. 'The old man and the boy won't go in there. Then you can get on to the bedrooms when they're out.'

'Aye, all right,' said Mrs Plottel, and added as if solicitous for the maid: 'Have you had your breakfast yet?'

The maid looked at her, blinked and said wearily: 'No, I'm just making it. What do you want?'

'Oh, just give me a cup of tea,' said Mrs Plottel. 'I was late, you see, and I hadn't time to take my breakfast.'

Sitting with the maid in the kitchen beside the freshly lit fire, warmed with it and the tea and a poached egg on hot toast, she began to feel ready again for her day's toil, the habit of work reasserting itself in her easily refreshed body. But as she swallowed the sweet, hot tea and felt the toast and egg, pleasantly salty, on her palate, she imagined her children at home, ragged in the fireless kitchen, squabbling over their share of the fried bread and the amount they should keep for their midday meal, while their father slept untroubledly in the room till two hours after they were gone to school.

'Well, come on,' said the maid, lighting a cigarette and getting out the bacon and eggs for her employers' breakfast. 'You'd better get out of here before the old girl gets on the prowl.'

Begun on the sitting-room before eight o'clock, helped by the maid to shift the furniture, Mrs Plottel found it a much harder and longer job than she had expected. Mrs Cowan came in when her husband was gone to his office and her boy was gone to the high school, and stood watching the work. She wore a dust-cap and an apron, and held a feather-duster, but she did no more than advise Mrs Plottel how to scrub the floor and wash the skirting-board, digressing occasionally from that into rambling gossip about her husband and her son and her neighbours, and the worries of not having nearly enough money to do the spring-cleaning properly and renovate the whole house.

'Yes,' said Mrs Plottel. 'It's a terrible thing the want of money.'

When she stopped for a light lunch at noon, she was so far behind the schedule she had worked out for herself that she wondered how she had ever thought she could do both the sitting-room and the dining-room in the morning, and it was with her fatigue slowly coming over her again, an exhausted despair before a task it would take unthinkably long toil to finish, that she returned to the first bedroom at half-past twelve. But once she had started again, her energy came back for the work as at a challenge, and sauntering in as she was sweating determinedly at it, with the maid doing odd lighter parts, Mrs Cowan said in a slow, friendly voice, with a college accent: 'You're doing fine, Mrs Plottel. You're a good worker when you get started, I'll say that for you.'

The words of encouragement spurred her on, and when she was given a cup of tea at half-past four she looked round the evidence of her industry with pride and pleasure. Then in a few minutes she began again alone, the maid going away to prepare dinner for the family, and her arms moved in slow weariness, habit taking control of her mindless, exhausted body.

'Well, that's the sitting-room and the two bedrooms done,' said Mrs Cowan, coming leisurely in as, painfully bent, Mrs Plottel was washing the skirting-board of the desolate dining-room, moving the cloth with a mechanical, blankly dogged thoroughness. 'I'll have dinner set in the sitting-room, and let you carry on here.'

At six o'clock, when the family were at dinner, she sat in the kitchen again with the maid, resting and eating. It was an effort for her to raise the spoon from her soup to her mouth, and sitting there at the table in relaxed content, she thought once more of her children away at the other end of the city, and looked up at the little clock on the mantelpiece, wearily happy that soon she would be back amongst them with money for a warm meal for them all.

She returned to the dining-room and worked there till after seven o'clock, and then Mrs Cowan came in and leaned against the doorway, fat and pampered and lazy, thought Mrs Plottel, regarding her employer with a sudden bitter envy. 'Oh, I think you might as well stop now, Mrs Plottel, and get away home,' she said.

Straightening gladly from her scrubbing, Mrs Plottel pushed back the straggling, damp hair from her throbbing forehead, and felt in that return to an erect position every bone in her body ache and all her muscles dead in weariness. 'You could hardly finish this tonight, anyway,' said Mrs Cowan, coming in and walking round the room examining the skirting-board. 'And you've the spare bedroom and the back-room still to do. You might as well leave this till tomorrow, and take another day to it altogether.'

Thinking of the money coming to her in a moment, and of the children waiting on it even now, Mrs Plottel took off her apron. The bus would take less than twenty minutes to cover the eight miles into the city, and a tram would take her the other two miles right to her tenement in a few minutes. She would be home earlier than she had said, and the children would not have the chance to get impatient. Within half an hour their hunger would be appeased and the empty larder filled for another day.

'I'll look out some old suits of Eric's,' said Mrs Cowan. 'There might be one or two things would do one of your boys. I'm sorry I've nothing for any of your girls. But I'm sure there must be some old things of my own I could give you. Are you needing shoes?'

'Well, I haven't any pair that's very good,' said Mrs Plottel. 'Anything you have would be welcome, Mrs Cowan, thank you.'

'I'll look them out tomorrow then,' said Mrs Cowan. She yawned, patting her mouth. 'Oh my, I was up too early this morning! It's been a long day. It's a tiring business, this spring-cleaning, but it's got to be done.'

She moved towards the door, and Mrs Plottel followed her expectantly. 'Come into the kitchen,' said Mrs Cowan, 'and Annie can give you a cup of tea to warm you up before you go. It's raining bad now. Sleet it is, really. Spring is going to be late this year.' Her apron in her hand, Mrs Plottel walked tiredly after her to the kitchen.

'Annie, give Mrs Plottel a cup of tea and something,' said Mrs Cowan, putting her head round the door, and turning with a friendly smile she ushered Mrs Plottel in.

Left alone with the maid, Mrs Plottel gossiped for ten minutes over her tea and ham sandwiches. But her mind was not on what she was saying, for every moment she was expecting Mrs Cowan to come in with her purse and pay her. When nothing happened after quarter of an hour, she supposed the woman did not want to pay her in front of the maid, and impatient to be home she rose and put on her coat and hat.

'Well, I'll away,' she said to the maid. 'See you tomorrow.'

'Cheery-bye,' said the maid, picking up her twopenny novelette again, and moving in closer to the fire.

'Good night,' said Mrs Plottel.

When she got into the hall, she unbuttoned her coat and loitered over buttoning it up again. She could hear Mrs Cowan talking in her lazy, rambling voice in the sitting-room, and for a moment she was irritated at the delay. Clearing her throat, she coughed, and looked hopefully towards the sitting-room door. With the calming of a fear she had barely admitted, she saw Mrs Cowan come out of the sitting-room, her large vanderbilt bag in her hand.

'Oh, by the way, Mrs Plottel,' she said brightly, 'I usually pay you today, but the smallest I have is a note. I'll leave it till tomorrow and give you two days' money then, since you're coming in again to finish the job anyway. That'll be all right, won't it?'

'Yes,' said Mrs Plottel blankly, so suddenly confronted with an outcome she had never expected that her brain would not work.

'Here, I'll show you out,' said Mrs Cowan, moving forward with helpful friendliness. 'It's a pity you didn't bring an umbrella. It's raining heavy now.'

Thoughtlessly, Mrs Plottel followed her to the door, and before she realized what she had done she was outside the house, with Mrs Cowan's bland farewell still in her ears. It was only when she got to the foot of the avenue and reached the bus stop on the main road that she understood what she had done. Standing hopelessly there, with no money for a bus, she was furious at herself, at Mrs Cowan, and then at herself again. If she had only expected it, she thought, she would have asked for her bus fare home anyway; or if Mrs Cowan had only let her know before she had her last cup of tea in the kitchen, she would have borrowed something from the maid. But, most of all, her anger was caused by the realization that she had been so slow-witted that she had meekly turned and let herself be put outside without even trying to explain that she had no money for her bus home. Then, unable to continue blaming herself, she was bitter against the smiling thoughtlessness of these people who lived in seven-roomed houses and had plenty of money, so polite that they could be sorry you hadn't an umbrella when it was raining, but never think of lending you one, never think you hadn't a penny for the bus home.

Turning citywards along the dark, gravel road of the suburb, she felt the sharp east wind pierce her shoddy coat, the chilly sleet blown full in her face, and the small, fine-edged pebbles cut into the soles of her shoes, hurting her tired feet. Her limbs heavy and aching after her long day's work, she would not think of the ten miles' walk before her, but the rain again soaked into her shoes, and she knew she would be drenched and ready to collapse long before she was even right into the city. And away at the other end of it her family were waiting, expecting her to be coming back with money in her pocket and warm fish and chips, in a vinegar-smelling parcel, under her arm.

'It'll be a fine drop for the old boy anyway,' she muttered bitterly to herself, plodding heavily on, her head down against the wind, and the empty trams and buses moved past her with swift aimfulness on the lonely, rain-gleaming road, on into the city and home.

Thoughtless

When their mother died, Plottel's father and uncles, wondering how much they would get, gathered again in the house where they fought together as boys. Their only sister, who after her marriage stayed next door to the old woman and daily attended her, acted as hostess, and the six brothers questioned her furtively, but she told them all she had no idea how much money there was. So six heads were busy working out what the accumulated dividends from the Co-operative Society should come to, and trying to guess the value of the insurance policies. The five brothers who had visited their mother about a dozen times in twenty years became fidgety to think how easily their sister could cheat them, and when the family riot which always arose when they met under one roof was ended by their departing separately, each in a fury at the selfishness of the others, the hostess was left alone with her eldest brother. He was a tramway inspector, and the spinsters of the parish thought him the 'nicest' of the Plottels—which was high praise, for the Plottels were locally considered a fine old family.

What he and his sister said when they were alone cannot now be known, but the other Plottels made a guess. Each told his suspicions to his wife, boasting of his acuteness in having them, only to find her jeer at him that for all he thought himself so smart he had marched out in a rage and left those two twisters to plot alone together.

To decry the cleverness of a Plottel male is a dangerous
thing, and the indiscreet wife provoked a tirade of insults
from the husband she mocked, followed by an aloof
silence which allowed him to keep the money righteously
to himself when it came, since he wasn't on speaking
terms with her.

The complaint of the poorer Plottels—and in spite of
their parochial reputation the Plottels were mainly a
paupered crew—was that those who most needed the
money got the least. It was declared among them, when
they spoke to each other in the kinship of feeling cheated,
that the tramway inspector, who had no children, had got
fifty pounds and the sister forty-five. But Plottel's uncle
round the corner, with ten children and a wife who had
so burdened him with debt that he had long ago become
tired of debt-collectors accosting him at the gate every
pay-day and given up his work to live on the charity of
the parish, got five pounds, which lasted him less than a
week.

Plottel's father was given eleven pounds, and went into
a theatrical temper at the insignificance of it, although his
total earnings were a pound a week from insurance
canvassing which he did in default of those revue-tours
regularly promised but never given him. He almost spoke
to his wife again, until he remembered he was treating her
with silent contempt, and so he was left with only the four
walls and his frightened family to rage at. For a moment
he made to tear the notes and throw them in the fire, just
to show what he thought of his brother and sister and
their filthy money. But he crumpled them instead and
pitched them across to a corner of the dresser, and then
when nobody was looking he hid them inside a small tin
box on the mantelpiece.

After he bought himself boots and an overcoat and a
new suit, he had about half the money left; and since he
gave her none of it, his wife went to the hiding place and

took a little every week. She saw everything he did, even when she seemed deliberately not looking at him, and she was so well used to his subterfuges that she unscrupulously explored his pockets and all the places he hid his money when he had any. Then, when he was out, teaching the children to scorn him, she laughed with them at his vanity making him assert he kept them all in the lap of luxury and didn't get enough attention and respect.

When he saw the money dwindle, Mr. Plottel took it out of the tin box and kept it in a purse which he carried always with him and put under his pillow at night. In a short time the purse too was empty, and he threw it into a drawer of rubbish.

The youngest child was later given the tin box to play with, and opening and shutting it in the pleasure of digital operations he thrust scraps of paper into it, pulling them out to shove them in again. 'I've got money,' he said as his father stood near him shaving in the kitchen. 'You used to have money in here, didn't you?'

Mr. Plottel, sneezing with the lather he always managed to brush up into his nostrils, turned and gaped at the child, and understood that not only his wife but the whole family had known where he first hid the money. 'You've said it,' he said, spitting in the sink. 'Used to have. But the man who could keep money in this house…'

'You made a damned good effort to keep it,' said Mrs. Plottel, stoking the fire with damp potato peelings. 'You made sure you gave none away.'

'It went just the same,' said Mr. Plottel. 'As soon as my back was turned.'

'It went on your back, you mean,' said Mrs. Plottel. 'On your own back, the same as always.'

'You'll be telling me next that you got nothing,' said Mr. Plottel.

'I had to take what I got,' said Mrs. Plottel. 'And God knows that wasn't much.'

'It's a millionaire you should have married,' said Mr.
Plottel.

'And that wouldn't have been you,' retorted his wife.

'Oh, would it not?' cried Mr. Plottel, as if he were
wronged in not being rated a millionaire.

The child stopped playing and stared with uncertain
fear at his parents, recognising in his mother's tone and
in the shout of his father's rhetorical question the setting
to their frequent quarrels. Open-mouthed and shaking he
moved away from his father and sidled into a corner
behind his mother.

'Well, I don't think so somehow,' said Mrs. Plottel.
'God knows you never had much. But what you do get,
goes on yourself. Every time. The rest of us can want.
Maybe you expect me to keep this house and your family
on nothing.'

'I bought what I needed,' shouted Mr. Plottel, fiercely
lathering his chin with a straggle-haired brush. 'I've got
to look after myself. I get damn little attention from you.
You're too damned lazy. And bloody stupid as well. It
wouldn't matter how much you got. A bloody spendthrift,
that's all you are.'

'It's kind of hard to be a spendthrift when you don't
get any money to spend,' said Mrs. Plottel, fondling the
head of the child come timidly clutching at her side. 'As
soon as you do get a little money, off you go and put it
on your back. Number one comes first with you all the
time.'

'I've got to look smart in my business,' said Mr. Plottel,
stirring his brush in the shaving mug, straightening with
pride as he mentioned his business, the word alone
sufficient stimulus for him again in a daydream to see
himself triumphant in a glorious limelight destiny.

'And what is your business?' asked Mrs. Plottel.

Having no precise answer ready, and hearing her
begin, in the advantage of his silence, to retail the history

of their married life and assert he hadn't given her a proper wage for ten years, Mr. Plottel, his chin bearded with still unrazored lather, threw half a loaf at her offending calm in an oathful fury, and the child began to cry.

With his legacy spent, he was again reduced to the little he earned by insurance canvassing, selling household goods on commission round the doors, and tracing debt-defaulters for moneylenders. Although it was now many years since he last appeared on the stage, he still talked as if he were only briefly and accidentally, through the conspiracy of freemasons, out of that theatrical work which was his proper and splendid career, a career far from being over as his wife slightingly declared, but just about to begin. When he was unexpectedly offered a place in a small touring company, he left the moneylender to find someone else to trace his defaulters, and practising old speeches, changing his voice to make his monologue sound a dialogue, he happily packed his bags. But he came back in a fortnight, ranting that he was an artiste, not an errand-boy or a stage-carpenter as well, and so Mrs. Plottel understood that once again his talent had been misused if not indeed unrecognised.

Back in the city to canvass for anything from insurance policies to fancy pencils, Mr. Plottel—who said he was the best canvasser in Glasgow, and implied he was the more to be admired therein since he also insisted canvassing wasn't his proper line—found his commission so small that he couldn't afford to give his wife anything. Mrs. Plottel then pawned the overmantel, sold the furniture article by article, and spied through the keyhole when she heard the ragwife come up the stair to see if it were coppers or crockery were being given in exchange for old garments and woollen rags. If it were crockery, she did not answer the ragwife's knock, but kept her precious bundle till the woman with coppers came.

So began one of the longest and worst periods of the family's poverty, while the mother gathered her children like chicks around her, leaving her husband to go on alone in the silence he had begun, serving without a word to him such meals as could be put together, and without a word Mr. Plottel would hungrily watch her and sit down immediately at the place set for him. He always ate alone, partly because he made so much noise with his defective false teeth that the sensitive children, who didn't like his company anyway, preferred to wait in their hunger rather than appease it at once by sitting down beside him, and partly because he was always so impatient to eat that a single meal had to be hastily prepared to satisfy him first.

But the children, because of their intelligence, were popular with the spinsters who taught them in the parish school, and noticing their increasing bootless shabbiness and malnutrition the spinsters gossiped among themselves. Soon, after mass or benediction or some Catholic social evening, they gossiped to their married friends, even hinting to the tramway inspector's plump and benevolent wife, whose childless comfort made them the more sympathetic for the many ill-clad and ill-fed nephews and nieces to whom they felt, for all they admired her parochial energy, she did not attend with the interest and generosity proper to a relative and a churchworker. Then in the week before Christmas Plottel himself, with the crust of a slice of bread fried in margarine in his hand, opened the door to a rhythmical knocking and saw on the landing a grocer's boy with a large basket, covered with sacking, at his feet.

'Plottel's?' said the grocer's boy.

Plottel bit the crust and stared with wondering hunger at the basket.

'Is this Plottel's?' repeated the grocer's boy impatiently.

Plottel nodded to the small nameplate, easily overlooked beside the door. 'Can't you read?' he asked, and looked again and more hungrily at the crammed-seeming basket. Mrs. Plottel came forward in slow curiosity from the kitchen to see what was going on. When she saw the basket she gaped.

'Plottel's order,' said the grocer's boy, touching his cap to her.

Mrs. Plottel looked from the basket to him, and looked down at the basket again. 'Bring it in,' she said suddenly jerking her head to motion him and looking like a penniless gambler determined to take the risk of palming a card. With obvious effort the boy raised the basket and entered. Plottel and his wife followed him into the kitchen, questioning each other with their eyes in speechless amazement. When the basket was emptied Mrs. Plottel gave the boy all the money she had, four-pence received that afternoon for rags.

Jabbering in loud excitement the children clustered round the unusually packed table, struggling against the attempts of their elder sister, a grave religious-minded girl of twelve, to force her way to the front, and grabbing at the bags and parcels to tear them open in impatient exploration.

'Mother,' said the timid jostled girl, 'you shouldn't have taken it. It must be a mistake.'

'Well, it's their mistake,' said Mrs. Plottel, who had long decided scrupulous honesty was too expensive for her to practise. 'And anybody who can afford all that can afford to lose it, too.'

Leaning against the dresser she watched her family complete a rapid survey of the contents of the basket.

'Ach, this is only sugar!' 'Look, currant bun!' 'What's this?'

'Rice,' said the eldest girl, working her elbow like a piston.

'Pooh, margarine!'

'Butter,' corrected the girl, almost right at the front, and pulling the fingers of one hand nervously now with those of the other in her conflict between a fear wherein she foresaw her mother in jail for stealing and her excitement at seeing so many provisions. 'Don't you know butter when you see it?'

'Ach, it's all the same,' said her brothers.

'It's not all the same!' cried the girl, her morbid worry conquered by her desire to show she knew something about groceries.

'Eggs!' 'Cheese!' 'Ugh, this is only lentils!' 'Biscuits!' 'Gingerbread!' 'Pickles!' 'That's only bread!' 'Tch, oatmeal!' 'Oh, look, a tin of pineapples!' 'Tea, tea, more tea!' 'Apple jelly, strawberry jam, cocoa, grapenuts!' 'Ugh, haricot beans! I thought it was something!' 'Ham!'

'That's not ham, it's bacon,' shouted the nervous girl in immediate pleasure, wholly happy now she could show off her superior knowledge.

The floor was littered with the discarded wrappings of provisions.

'There's no milk,' said Mrs. Plottel coming forward to see exactly what there was, and trying to calculate how much the lot had cost. 'They might have thought of putting in a tin of condensed milk.'

'But mother,' said the eldest girl, worried again in her fading excitement, 'how do you know it's for us? You shouldn't have taken it. You don't know who it might have been for.'

'It's ours now,' said Mrs. Plottel grimly.

'But mother,' repeated the girl, nervously pulling her fingers again.

'Mother your granny,' said Mrs. Plottel, marshalling the goods into a semblance of order.

The next day the eldest girl was given by the nun in charge of the school a sealed letter to take home to her mother. The letter asked them all to pray for the donor of a basket of provisions they should have received.

'What's a donor?' asked Mrs. Plottel, holding the letter

as if it had an infection on it.

'A lady,' said the girl gravely. 'It's an Italian word,'

'I wonder who it is,' muttered Mrs. Plottel. 'My God, if it's that big fat lump ... Ach, what does it matter! Even if it is, she can afford it.'

But the workings of parochial charity were not finished. A few evenings later, when Mr. Plottel had gone out as usual to a music-hall where he would be admitted for nothing on showing his card, and Mrs. Plottel sat half asleep before a fire stoked with dross and refuse, there was a solemn knock at the door. The children stopped quarrelling and Mrs. Plottel jolted to a scared wakefulness. It was their custom, caused by the troublesome visits of factor's clerks and debt-collectors, never to open the door unless the person knocking was insistent and plainly determined to get an answer. So everyone sat perfectly still and quiet in order not to give the would-be visitor the unnecessary encouragement of hearing people within the house. The solemn knock came again, deepening their hush, and realising that so late in the evening it could hardly be anyone come to demand money owing, Mrs. Plottel rose with experienced noiselessness and tried to spy through the keyhole. Then, after waiting till the knock was repeated to make it seem that the third one was the first to her hearing, she turned back to the kitchen and coughed there, making a long-practised rustle as if she were coming along the lobby, and turned again to open the door. Two tall bowlered men in black overcoats darkened the threshold.

'Mrs. Plottel?' said one, and each raised his bowler half-an-inch.

Mrs. Plottel nodded, too startled to speak, and stood blocking the entrance.

'We're from the Saint Vincent de Paul Society,' said the one who had already spoken,and his partner bowed supportingly.

'Oh, come in!' said Mrs. Plottel, assuming the graciousness of a lady. Her respect for the Church making her immediately courteous even to the lay emissaries of a charitable organisation connected with it, she was willing to let them enter that kitchen from which, because of its untidy and usually unclean poverty, all callers were normally excluded. The dark representatives of benevolence went clumsily past her as she gestured them, each taking off his hat and nervously smoothing his hair with a large gloved hand. Too embarrassed to go any further when they saw the littered confusion of the penniless kitchen, they stuck shyly at the doorway to it.

'We were told,' said the one who was evidently to be the spokesman of the mission, 'I mean, we were advised, er, we were recommended ...'

'Yes?' said Mrs. Plottel, holding her head high, standing facing them again with her back to the kitchen, and with one hand behind her signalling the children to be quiet, although they were too interested and in awe to move.

'I mean, we've come to see you,' plunged the speaker. His silent partner nodded approval of the statement. Mrs. Plottel almost retorted 'So I see,' but checked her natural sarcasm and bowed.

'You see, we were told you were—you were—you were having a hard time of it just now,' hurried the spokesman, running the fingers of one hand round the crown of his bowler held against his chest. 'We were asked to see if you could be helped—I mean, if we could help you. I mean ...'

'Yes?' said Mrs. Plottel encouragingly.

'Your husband isn't working?' he fired suddenly, toning the statement for a question.

'No,' said Mrs. Plottel, who since she got nothing out of it refused to call her husband's irregular canvassing working, although Mr. Plottel himself thought it very hard work. 'I've been all over Partick, Whiteinch, Govan,

Plantation and Kinning Park the day,' he would say in the evening. 'Up and down stairs, up and down stairs. And no bloody thanks for it.'

'You'll find it hard to feed and clothe your family?' said the spokesman slowly, as if confronted with data from which inferences must be made with great caution.

'Occasionally,' said Mrs. Plottel gently.

'Does he drink?' darted the speaker, nervously fingering the doorjamb.

'Oh, no,' said Mrs. Plottel, drawing out the vowels.

'You see, we have to ask that, you know, just to make sure,' mumbled the speaker, embarrassedly apologetic. 'Well, you know, there's no use helping people, trying to help people, if the man would just drink it.'

'No,' said Mrs. Plottel.

'He's all right to you—'n' to the children?'

'Oh, well, yes,' answered Mrs. Plottel not quite surely.

'He's all right really? Just, he's not working, is that it?' asked the spokesman with a strange hopefulness, as if reluctant to hear Mr. Plottel had any definite and constant failings.

'That's it,' Mrs. Plottel, never an argumentative woman, agreed readily. 'He was all right when he had a job. It's all because he'd never stick in one. The stage, the stage, all the time. And of course that work never lasts. It's no use unless you're at the very top. Where he never was near. And now he can't get a proper job. Men won't give him a job just for him to leave when the fancy takes him.

'I see,' said the spokesman. 'You're quite sure he doesn't drink?'

'Oh, no; he never touches it. It's just he won't stick in one job. Throws them away for a month with a revue or something like that. The head man in the insurance said it was a great pity the stage had got into his blood. He could have had his own office today, he said, if he had only been content to stay in the business. Oh, but that was years ago!'

'Except for that he's not bad?' said the spokesman.

'Oh well, no,' said Mrs. Plottel, beginning to tire of the questioning which seemed unprofitable to her. 'He's all right when he's working. Just, he's a wee bit—well, a wee bit selfish.... Thoughtless, really. That's all,' she hurried, having found the word. 'He's just thoughtless.'

'Hm,' grunted the hitherto silent partner in the mission.

Mrs. Plottel stared at the two men, waiting the next move, and they stared at the floor, one fingering his bowler, the other caressing the jamb of the doorway. Then the one who had done all the talking slowly brought out a wallet from his inside pocket, and gave Mrs. Plottel two pounds notes from it. Mumbling words she was too excited to hear, he turned from her, putting on his hat, and in rapid embarrassment, like a soldier caught out of step and hurrying to create the semblance of coincidence, his partner imitating him. When she had shown them out, Mrs. Plottel staggered back into the kitchen laughing merrily, and banging the door behind her she leaned against it, waving the notes. The children, already mobilised, jumped quarrellingly round her to snatch the notes as she flourished them teasingly just above their hands.

'How much did you get?' they cried. 'Oh, mother, get us fish and chips!'

'What's the time?' said Mrs. Plottel. She lifted her coat from the couch, her hat from the floor, and looked for her shoes while the boys cried: 'I'll go!' 'I'll go!' 'I'll go!' 'I'll go!'

'It's all right,' she said, easing her shoes from where they were jammed under the fender. 'I know what I want myself.'

She came back with the fish and chips they wanted, and two bottles of Guinness for herself. When Mr. Plottel came in, the bottles were empty and hidden and the wrappings of the fish and chips burned. But none of them had remembered to put away the salt cellar, and the eldest girl, who with a fiction-bred fastidiousness had used a fork for her chips, had left it lying beside her plate. With the sharpness of experience Mr. Plottel stared at the salt and the fork, and looked round the room like a policeman. The next morning he spoke in a friendly tone to his wife, and told her his boots were needing mending.

'Will I just send them down?' he asked pleasantly, clearing the breakfast table for her.

Mrs. Plottel looked round at him, bewildered at the calm assurance of his implication that she could afford it, and many bitter charges confusedly phrased themselves in her head. Then turning away, in tired impartiality resignedly she said, 'Oh, I suppose you might as well.'

'I don't understand it,' she said to her family in the evening when as usual Mr. Plottel went out to a music-hall. 'He seems to smell money. Asks me can he send his boots down. Asks me, if you please! Meaning I pay. My money's for him, but his is for himself. Oh, he's great! But I wish I knew how he got to know!'

Continuing his friendly tone, Mr. Plottel said he needed a new shirt. When she bought him one and paid for the repair of his boots, and gave the grocer something on account that her credit might get a fresh lease, Mrs. Plottel had two half-crowns left. Looking at the coins unfamiliarly located in her purse, she muttered: 'They shouldn't have given me so much. What the hell use to me is their charity once in a blue moon? And you're all still needing boots. However, the old boy's provided for. I suppose that's all that matters.'

Clothes

Miss M'Kernan looked sideways at the boy, eyeing him up and down as she marked the four sums in his jotter correct. The ragged woollen jersey he wore was fastened loosely over his shoulder with a rusted safety-pin, the toes of his un-stockinged feet wriggled dirtily through cheap, torn sand-shoes, and when he turned and walked back to his desk, blushing with pride at being first out with the four sums correct, she saw the seat of his baggy trousers was thread-bare to a hole through which the crumpled tail of his shirt coyly peeped.

Tapping her blue correcting-pencil against the nail of her thumb, she looked round her well-disciplined class and gravely meditated. The boy was the fourth of the family to come under her tuition, and since she had found every one of them clever she had made a favourite of each during his year with her. But she had noticed an increasing shabbiness in them, and the condition of the latest member disturbed her benevolence.

'Appalling,' she said to herself. 'They're not even clean now.'

At playtime, talking in the corridor with the nun who was head mistress of the parish school, she remembered the boy and spoke of him.

'The only thing to do,' said Sister Evangeline, 'is to give him a form for boots and clothing from the Authority.

These children will never ask for one. I suppose it's because we're not long under the Authority, our people don't know of all its services.... Come with me now, and I'll give you a form.'

At four o'clock, when evening prayers were said and the children were marching out in an orderly double line, Miss M'Kernan lightly grasped the boy's arm and wheeled him over to a corner of the room. Fidgeting uneasily, wondering what he had done wrong, the boy watched her go to her desk when the class was gone. But she did not bring out a strap. She brought out a pale-green paper, and beckoned him over with a commanding jerk of her head.

'Are those the only clothes you have?' she asked.

'Yes, miss,' he answered, red-faced.

'Is your father working?' she said.

'No, miss,' he mumbled, and hated her for her questions.

'I want you,' she said, 'to take this form home to your parents and get your father or mother to fill it up. You get that done, and bring it back to me tomorrow. Understand?'

'Yes, miss,' he answered, distrustfully taking the form, his big toe wriggling nervously through the hole in his left shoe. He didn't understand at all what it meant.

'You do that,' said Miss M'Kernan, 'and we'll see if we can get better clothes for you. And for James and Peggy, too.'

'Oh, and there's Tommy,' she added quickly. 'He's in the supplementary now, isn't he? But Martha and John have left school. I know that. Martha used to be a very good girl in my class. Tell her I was asking for her.'

When he gave the form to his mother at home, she opened it worriedly and looked with distaste at the headings and sub-headings and dotted lines for answers, and the three columns for a financial statement.

'Oh, I can't read that!' she cried. 'I can't make head nor

tail of it. In any case, it's your father that's to sign it, not me.'

But when Mr Plottel came in, he too read the form impatiently and demanded of no one in particular: 'What the hell do they want to know all this for?'

'To see if you really can't afford to get them clothes,' explained his wife.

'Aye, I know that,' said Mr Plottel, irritated that he should be insulted by having his rhetorical question taken as indicating obtuseness rather than the righteous wrath he felt against interfering strangers and inquisitive bureaucrats. 'And why should I tell them all my business?'

'If you had any business to tell ... ' taunted his wife. 'You fill it up, and let them get clothes from Bath Street. They'll never get them if they're waiting on you.'

'Oh, would they not?' said Mr Plottel, nodding his head in ironic appreciation and then snorting in contempt.

In a moment they were quarrelling as violently as usual, and Mr Plottel threw the pen savagely to the floor and refused to have anything more to do with the form.

When he was gone out for the evening his wife drew the pen out of the faded waxcloth and tried to bring the bent ends of the nib together again. Then laboriously, sighing every few minutes, she completed the form with the aid of the eldest boy, who wrote his father's signature at the foot, copying the theatrically distinctive flourishes of it from an insurance book.

The form was returned to Miss M'Kernan, and Sister Evangeline enclosed it in the wallet which was delivered twice weekly to the Education Offices. Three weeks later Mrs Plottel was instructed by an official letter to bring the children to the Normal School to be fitted with clothes. With difficulty she got the money for tram fares, and clutching the letter like a weapon in her hand, she arrived punctually at the end of the Cowcaddens with the three boys and their sister.

A bright-voiced girl led them to a waiting-room, and obedient to her smiling request they sat down timidly together on a long form against the wall of a large hall with a bare wooden floor. Many people were already there, and in dismay the impatient children tried to work out with each other just how long it would take before it was their turn. With her hands in her lap, twisting the unasked-for letter, hot and flustered with the novelty of the trip, Mrs Plottel sat silently on the edge of the form and stared into unfurnished space.

As the morning drew near noon and they were still not appreciably nearer their turn, the eldest boy from the supplementary school began to blame his brother from the qualifying class for their being there at all.

'It's not my fault,' objected the boy. 'Miss M'Kernan gave me the form. I couldn't tell her to keep it.'

'Ach!' said his brother unreasoningly.

'Well, it's worth it,' argued the boy. 'We'll get suits. That's better than these old jerseys.'

'I'll bet you they're not good suits,' said his brother.

'Hold your tongue,' scolded Mrs Plottel. 'Do you want folk to hear you? Of course they'll be good suits.'

To get away from his dissatisfied brother, the boy from Miss M'Kernan's class walked round the room alone, pretending not to notice the other ragged children he passed in his circuit. He looked forward to getting a suit. He had never had new clothes before, except a cheap jersey twice a year, and the thought of a proper suit excited him. He had always wanted to be well-dressed and have no need to worry about his shirt being seen through a loose patch on the seat of his trousers.

'For heaven's sake, sit down you, and be at peace,' whispered his mother fiercely, when his circular route brought him back to the rest of the family. 'You make as much noise trapezing all round the room in those boots! You'd think you were Charlie Chaplin. Can't you see everybody looking at you!'

'They're not so well-dressed themselves,' muttered the
boy, angry to think that his large boots, an uncle's
cast-offs, had made him seem ludicrous in his walk round
the room. But afraid that his mother was correct, he sat
down again on the form and stared gloomily at the huge
unpolished casings of his feet.

'It's the boots,' he complained. 'My feet aren't big. I'd
have been better with my sand-shoes on.'

'Aye, and your toes sticking through them,' gibed his
mother.

'Look!' whispered the eldest boy, nudging him in the
ribs with malicious vigour. 'You see that? I told you they
wouldn't be good suits!'

Looking where his brother indicated he saw two
schoolboys come back into the room to rejoin their
mother. They were dressed alike in dark-grey Norfolk
suits, each with an untidy brown-paper parcel under his
arm containing his old clothes. Flushed and uneasily
clumsy in the creased newness of the old-fashioned suits
and heavy thick-soled boots, they lumbered over to their
brown-shawled mother.

'They're giving them all those suits!' muttered the boy,
in tardy understanding to his brother, dismayed to near
tears after his dreams of splendour. 'Everybody will know
where we got them!'

His expectation of appearing well clad and prosperous,
in a suit that no one would know came from charity, was
ended in bitterness, but his brother was irrationally
jubilant that his words had come true.

Their turn came next, at the very moment when the boy
would gladly have left the building and worn his patched
trousers for ever. He was led to a dim, empty cubicle, and
there a brisk young man brought him heavy combinations
first. Stripped to get them on, he felt with loathing the
coarse, loose-woven wool next his skin, and saw nothing

wrong with his tattered shirt. It at least didn't tickle him in this grossly intimate way.

The new shirt, too, was heavy, with a dark-blue pattern, exactly the same as he had seen the boys in the waiting-room wear. Just like the kind carters have, he thought, and put it on in a struggling fury against Miss M'Kernan. When he had put on the trousers of thick, dark cloth, he found the stockings were of a heavy, rust-coloured wool. Easily he convinced himself they looked horrible. Then as he laced up the boots he saw there were small holes pierced in the uppers and arranged to form the initials E.A.G. Education Authority, Glasgow, he cried to himself, straightening for a moment rebelliously. Why don't they stamp it on the backside of the pants, too!

Scowling, he surveyed the Norfolk jacket before he put it on, and with a sneer at his own foolish hopes he thought of the kind of suit he had expected to get, a suit with a jacket that had lapels and no silly belt; a suit the same as Tony Pelosi wore—but Tony Pelosi's father had an ice-cream shop.

'Nobody wears Norfolk suits these days,' he complained to himself, his heart a smouldering core of anger against Miss M'Kernan. 'Nobody wears them except the folk that get them from the Authority. Everybody will know we're poor.'

The thought of appearing before his classmates in this new Norfolk suit made him feel he would rather be dead. All the dunces who couldn't get a sum right and couldn't do a composition, all the copiers who pleaded with him to let them see his jotter, all of them would get the chance to mock him. And he was rebellious against the world at the knowledge that they, for all he could despise them in the classroom, would have the superiority outside, and be free from the glaring stigma of an unfashionable suit made to a common pattern, and given to the poor by the

Education Authority.

On the way home, carrying his old clothes wrapped in brown paper given him in the cubicle, he asked his elder brother why the boots were stamped E.A.G.

'Oh, that's in case the old folks try to pawn them to buy the red wine,' said his brother wisely. 'The pawnshop won't take them with the stamp on them.'

The sordidness of the idea made him feel the boots heavier and more repulsive than ever.

'I don't believe it,' he said, and spoke no more to his brother. But then in his silence, thinking of the trip they had just made, he remembered that coming down in the tram and now again going home in it, he had been glad when his mother went into the lower deck with his sister and let the boys go upstairs. He had been glad because he was ashamed of her shabby coat and bad shoes, and the unwilling realization of his own snobbery irritated him.

For two days he put off wearing the Norfolk suit, although he was content in the end to wear the boots, since his mother had nothing else to give him for his feet. And then she insisted he wear the suit and leave off the jersey she was tired darning. Unhappily he put it on, and loitered on the way to school so that he would not have time to be seen in the playground with it. He reached the yard just as the bell was rung and slinked to the rear of his line. Blushing and stiff, he marched in with conscious bravery, hoping nobody noticed what he was wearing.

At playtime he took the jacket off, and let it be used to mark one of the goalposts in the yard as he played at football with the others. It was the jacket most annoyed him. The trousers looked ordinary, and he was sure nobody could ever notice the initials stamped on the boots.

Marching upstairs at the end of the interval, he carried the jacket over his arm. As the class-rank rounded the first landing to go on up the next flight, Sister Evangeline stood there clapping her hands rhythmically. 'Left, right, left, right,' she called firmly, her innocent eyes behind her glasses watching the discipline of the lines. Red-faced at the noise his heavy boots were making, the boy came to pass her.

'Plottel!' she called sharply, her voice loud and clear. 'The Authority gave you that jacket to put on. Put it on!'

Halted in embarrassment at her ringing tone, the boy was at first too distracted at being publicly named to take in the sense of her words. Then as it reached him, he felt his face hot at the revealing of his shame to a crowded stairway, a revealing of it brought about by the very subterfuge he had meant to conceal it.

'That's what you got the jacket for,' said Sister Evangeline in a tone of chilling common sense. 'Not to carry over your arm.'

Sullenly, slowly obedient, conscious of the turned heads and gaping mouths of his classmates, the boy shook out the jacket and wriggled his arms into the sleeves as he marched heavy-footed in rank back to the classroom. He saw a girl in front of him, wearing a bright new frock, grin over her shoulder at his humiliation. Then his sight was blurred by tears of helpless anger and the bitterness of a vanity he knew was doomed to derision, and he wanted to tear off the jacket, to trample it ruinously underfoot and return to his ragged jersey, his baggy trousers and his torn sand-shoes. They were at least his own, to wear when he liked, old, familiar and paid for, unstamped and unnoticed.

Brothers

In the long summer holidays he had nothing to do all day after he had delivered the milk in the mornings. He was bored, and would rather have been back at school. Sentenced again to the tenements for the dreary summer, he borrowed books daily from the public library beyond the Stinkie Burn and counted the empty weeks still ahead. The blue sky between the remote roofs of the tenements coaxed him out of *King Solomon's Mines* one morning, and he wandered across the main road to the level waste ground in the hinterland of the backstreets, an aimless vitality urging him to action. On the quarry that flanked the Territorial Drill Hall a gang of boys were playing with a full size newly-dubbined ball. He stood on the margin of the game, afraid to ask them to let him join in, for in the tradition of the tenements the two sides of the street never mixed. The main road between them was a line that could be crossed as the border between neighbouring countries could be crossed, but the mere crossing of it did not necessarily lead to any welcome from the foreigners on the other side. He knew the gang but slightly; under the leadership of Shoe McAuchan, a burly bruiser of thirteen, they formed a nomadic tribe that rejected all intruders on their hunting-grounds. They were coarser than his own comrades, and he had a furtive admiration for the insolence of their manners, the violence of their swearing, and for their fame as bare-fist fighters.

The ball ran out of play and he chased it like a sportive dog that will run after anything in motion.

'Hey you! do you want a game?' shouted McAuchan patronisingly.

'What do you want to give him a game for?' demanded Knox in a surly voice. 'He's not on our side of the street.'

'No, but he's Johnny Plottel's young brother,' said McAuchan. 'That's good enough. And you've a man more than us anyway.'

McAuchan had his way as usual, and Plottel gladly took the position allotted him. He felt released from solitary confinement, allowed to enter the world again and take part in its activities, though it offended his vanity to be accepted by the gang merely because of his brother. He had no idea how John, long expelled by his own side of the street for his domineering manner and his cheating, had managed to join the McAuchan tribe, but he knew that he commonly assumed an air of toughness and worldly experience, and that he swore glibly in imitation of his elders; he had no doubt bluffed or bribed McAuchan into accepting him as a member. It was not the first time he had tried to attach himself to a neighbouring group, and it always ended the same way. Sooner or later the bluff would be found out or the bribe disowned. Sooner or later his brother would be thrown out, disgraced and despised, and he would be disgraced too.

His misgivings made him cautious with his new company. He was glad of it in the mornings when his brother was still delivering groceries for old Mr Munro, but he scrupulously avoided it in the afternoons, when his brother had finished his errands and joined the gang in the quarry. He could not bear to be anywhere near him, and he was unwilling to witness the challenge which he knew would arise—a challenge his brother always provoked by his ambition to be boss wherever he went, and from which, having provoked it, he always retreated with a foolish grin, shouting back defiance only when he was a safe distance away.

It came as he knew it would. He went to the quarry one morning when clouds were threatening to wash the dregs of the summer, and the gang were all there. The ball came out in the loose towards him as he approached, enticing him. He scampered happily to boot it, and McAuchan at once let out a menacing shout and warned him off. He looked up in surprise, dismayed at McAuchan's tone, and then defiantly kicked the ball back to McAuchan. It hit him on the stomach, and he went on his knees with a yelp of pain.

'You did that on purpose,' gasped McAuchan, getting slowly to his feet.

The very slowness of his rise was a threat that appalled Plottel, and he suddenly realised just how big McAuchan was and how strong he looked.

'I didn't,' he said defensively. 'I just kicked it. I didn't mean it to hit you.'

'Ach, he's yellow,' said a bandylegged boy with a scabby chin. He spat at Plottel's feet.

'Like his big brother,' said McAuchan contemptuously.

Plottel looked from one to the other in a panic. Cautiously he came back a step. He did not know what his brother had done to forfeit the friendship of the McAuchan gang and involve him too in their enmity. He did not need to know. It was sufficient to recognise he was in danger. The gang formed a ring round him, leaving McAuchan inside it too, facing him. He remembered then, as a fact peculiarly relevant to his situation, that McAuchan was respected in the main road and the back streets as a fighter who had been trained to box by his big brother, a professional flyweight. He had once knocked a boy right off his feet with an uppercut, and nobody would fight McAuchan after that. And now he was confronted with McAuchan facing up to him, his stance crouched, his left well forward, his whole attitude professional. Plottel raised his own fists to the pose of defence, and felt himself trembling. He was sick with fright, and yet he had time to notice that a nerve in his thigh was vibrating rapidly, and it puzzled him.

'So you want to fight?' jeered McAuchan, lowering his grimy coarse-grained fists, and derisively leaving Plottel in the position of the aggressor.

'It's you that wants to fight,' said Plottel, quickly dropping his guard. 'I don't want to fight.'

'I told you he was yellow,' commented the scabbyfaced boy in a gloomy disgust.

'Like your big brother, eh?' said McAuchan. 'Afraid you'll get hurt?'

'It would take more than you to hurt me,' retorted Plottel, wondering if McAuchan was offering him the chance to get out of it by bluster; and desperately eager to say the right thing without committing himself too far, he added defensively: 'Because my brother's afraid of you doesn't mean to say I am. Maybe he's a coward but I'm not!'

'Christ and we'll bloody soon see!' cried McAuchan, and he took up a fighting stance again.

Plottel stepped back, scared to the back of his neck; he saw he had misjudged it, he was not being offered any way out by talking. The very language McAuchan used frightened him, and his Catholic prejudices were shocked at his opponent's irreverent invocation of the Son of God. He scowled, trying hard to look a fighter, and he remembered Sister Agnes, taking his class for religious instruction during Holy Week, telling once again the story of the soldiers coming to seize Our Lord in the Garden of Gethsemane with lanterns and torches and weapons. And when he said unto them, Whom seek ye? they answered him, Jesus of Nazareth; and Jesus said unto them, I am he.

'Notice,' said Sister Agnes, 'Our Lord did not say I am him, because that's bad grammar. He said I am he, because the verb to be takes the same case after it as before it.'

He had a passing doubt if Our Lord spoke English at all, but he dared not say so to Sister Agnes. That was the Gospel according to St John, and it was because of John he was in this fight. He knew there was no way out, none that he could take; he knew there was only one thing to do, to go on and go in and stay in and keep on hitting. But he was cleaved with fear. There were two of him: one that sat inside, behind his eyes, and knew the only way to fight but had nothing more to do with the matter once it had pointed that way out to him; and another that was the visible, touchable self, the fists he could see clenched under his eyes, the feet he stood on, the whole miserable, cowardly, agonised body that had to do the fighting but didn't want to. He felt a third being clamber out of the depths of his terror and push the trembling body forward. He shaped up clumsily to McAuchan and they circled round, making a grim, silent mime of preparing to fight. The ring crowded in upon them, pushing Plottel towards his foe and shouting for action. The sky was far, away and the quarry the whole world. He retreated and veered as McAuchan, smiling with the lust of blood, closed slowly in on him. He saw the teeth bared, with brown streaks where they emerged from the red gums, saw the loose mouth taunting him in an engulfing grin, saw the small pale eyes measure him and watch for an opening. And still they circled round and not a blow was struck.

'Aw chuck the dancin,' groaned Scabby Ross impatiently. 'Hit him, Shoey, hit him. For Christ's sake, hit him.'

'Go on, Shoey! What are ye waitin for?' shouted McKay.

But still they circled.

'Aw Christ!' moaned Scabby Ross, and chanted in mockery of them both a backcourt circle song sung by children:

Here we go roon the ring-a-ring,
The jing-a-jing, the ring-a-ring,
Here we go roon the ring-a-ring,
Roon aboot Mary Matansie.

His chant was drowned in a surge of shouting and bawling; the gang swayed in a frantic clamour, encouraging their champion, swearing at his opponent, hungry for blood. Barely conscious of the noise around him, Plottel contemplated himself unsympathetically from a remote height and wondered how it would end. Then out of the shouting and jeering he heard clearly and sharply, rising unforgettably above the tumult, a vicious, venomous injunction.

'Kill the papish bastard!'

The words maddened him beyond discretion. To avenge himself for them, he rushed in against the lead of McAuchan's left, blindly ignoring the sparring paw that was meant to make him keep his distance. He did not care how much punishment he took so long as he hit McAuchan hard enough and often enough to draw blood. He was a damned soul, struggling amid alien powers in darkness, and he had to achieve redemption by blood. Only blood could wash away the insult.

Surprised by the wild attack, McAuchan yielded ground, and barking in anger and disappointment the ring broke behind him to allow him to recover. Vicariously

aggressive, it re-formed quickly and forced him into fight.
But he would not. He was weak, bewildered, and
ineffective. Plottel saw the state of his foe and rejoiced.
His God had taken vengeance for the and he was the
instrument. He went for the blood he wanted, realising
that McAuchan's uppercut was only a myth and that
McAuchan wasn't a boxer at all, he wasn't even a fighter.
Encouraged by the visible approach of victory, he kept on
punching McAuchan's nose till it bled. He kept close in
and jabbed him in the stomach as hard as he could.
Overwhelmed and routed, McAuchan gave up trying to
fight back. He held both hands in front of his bleeding
nose and wept convulsively. Then he grabbed Plottel
round the neck, fumbling to put a wrestler's grip on him.
Plottel kicked him unscrupulously on the ankle and
heaved him to the ground.

The ring broke completely and reassembled round its
fallen champion. Scabby Ross and McKay helped him to
his feet, Knox brushed his back, and Onnachie gave him
a dirty handkerchief for his bleeding nose.

Plottel turned slowly and walked away. The quarry
seemed vast, the nearest back street immeasurably
remote. Someone threw a stone after him. He turned
again and waited, his fists clenched, his face a defiant
scowl, and his belly throbbing like a steam-engine
gathering speed, but the gang looked silently back at him,
giving scowl for scowl. He went on his way towards the
safety of the backstreets and heard Knox shout after him,
Irish bastard. The words no longer bothered him; he had
learnt their value.

But his jersey was torn at the neck and shoulder where
McAuchan had wrestled with him at the end of the fight,
and when he went in for dinner his mother saw it.

'Do you think I've nothing else to do but get you a new
jersey every week?' she cried angrily. 'You've got your
jacket so as you can't wear it, and you're going to do the

same with your jersey. If you'd keep out of fights you wouldn't come in with your clothes half off your back. You're a quarrelsome little devil.'

He stayed in the house in the afternoon, finishing *King Solomon's Mines*, turning his back on the sun that had enticed him out to an empty victory. His mother went out and he was alone. Halfway through the afternoon John came in. As soon as he heard him, he felt himself bristling, and could read no longer. His dislike had become a festering hatred, and it upset him even to be in the same room as his brother.

'What were you saying about me?' demanded John, standing over him and rudely knocking the book from his hand.

'Here, that's a library book,' said Plottel fiercely, jumping to his feet. 'Don't you throw it about like that. It's me that's got to take it back.'

'To hell with you and your books, you little bookworm,' said John, sneering in contempt. 'What were you saying about me to McAuchan?'

'And what would I be saying about you?' he hedged.

'You told Shoey McAuchan I was a coward, didn't you?' shouted John, his face red with anger.

'What if I did?' he asked. 'You start a fight and then leave me to finish it. What would you like me to call you?'

'When did you ever fight for me?' said John. 'Christ, I'd be hard up if I had to let a crank like you do my fighting What would you be doing, fighting for me, when I could knock your lights out with one hand?'

'Maybe that's why you couldn't fight McAuchan with two,' he taunted. 'You left it for me.'

'Oh, so you're the fighting man of the family, are you?' cried John, sticking his nose against his brother's face because he knew it maddened him beyond selfcontrol. 'You can beat Shoey McAuchan any time you like, uppercuts don't bother you, eh? You can beat a fellow that's been trained to box!'

'I left him flat on his back anyway,' he answered hotly. 'And he didn't call me a coward.'

'Are you trying to call me one?' said John, and without warning hit him suddenly across the eyes with outspread fingers.

'I don't want to fight!' he sobbed, one hand over his smarting eyes. 'I don't want to fight! I've had enough fighting!'

John pushed him on the chest, so that he stumbled back and almost fell over. He came back again madly, but he was too wretched to fight. His eyes were watering with pain, and as he hit out wildly his brother punched him where and as he liked, grinning with relish at having made him weep.

He gave it up and ran through to the empty kitchen, where the remnants of the frugal dinner still littered the table.

'I'm tired fighting,' he wailed. 'Catholic and Protestant and Scotch and Irish! I'm tired fighting! We don't even know if we are Irish, our name isn't Irish. Why should I have to fight Protestants because we're Catholics? Why should I have to fight the Scotch because they call me Irish? Why should I have to fight your fights because you're my brother?'

His brother, sauntering into the kitchen at his heels, listened complacently to the weeping rhetoric.

'Go on, cry! cry, baby, cry!' he said, delighted at the spectacle that vindicated his superiority.

Blackleg

Mr Bulloch, a Corporation tram-driver, was so big and stout that they called him 'Bullock' in the depot. His wife was a massive woman, and his two sons were big and fat. There was an atmosphere of stolid strength, of aloofness and security, about the family. When they were twelve, the two boys went to a higher grade school, and their mother talked like a west-end lady. She meant them to go to the university after that and become engineers or doctors or schoolmasters, and with that high ambition she didn't like them to play with the other children who would leave school at fourteen and become errand-boys.

In the back-court, the elder of the two boys was feared for his height and strength, and he always got his own way without having to do much bullying. But one evening in the spring his domineering interference provoked one of the fighting Plottels to oppose him, and he so thoroughly buffeted the foolhardy boy that the others, jostling round the fight, began to murmur against his cold-blooded brutality. Cornered and in tears, Plottel punched ineffectively up at the looming bulk of his enemy.

'Away and fight somebody your own size!' shouted a girl righteously from the back of the hostile throng.

'I'll fight who I like,' retorted Bulloch, and turning again he hit Plottel hard on the ear with a large rough-skinned fist.

His sight blurred by tears and his head ringing with that blow, Plottel wriggled out of the corner and stood tremblingly clear.

'I'll fight your young brother if I can't fight you,' he cried. 'He's my age. You're not.'

'Come on, James,' said the elder Bulloch magnanimously, gesturing his brother from the fringe to the ring. 'You give him the same as you saw me do.'

Red-faced, drawing back and muttering something indistinctly, the younger Bulloch refused. And from that evening the strength of the brothers was no longer respected. Without an opponent to match against the elder Bulloch, the boys jeered at him safely from a distance, calling him Big Chief Sitting Bull, and the younger one shared his elder's disgrace.

Then, in the summer, the hostility and mockery that had arisen against the family in the squabbles of schoolboys spread to it on the adult level. The General Strike was declared, and the city was disorganized and excited. When it was seen that Mr Bulloch went on driving a tram, the whole street murmured against him.

'Imagine him, born and reared in the Butney, helping a gang of students to break the Strike!' said Mrs Reid in anger. 'Maybe he thinks he's a toff because he's got two boys at the high school. I know what I'd like to tell him!'

'Ach, and his wife's not much better,' said Mrs Farquhar. 'Her and her fine airs and her Kelvinside voice! I knew her before she came here, before she was ever married, and believe you me, she wasn't far from the gutter when she was born.'

'Deserting his own class like that!' said Mrs Houston. 'He should be ashamed of himself.'

In those sunlit mornings of May, the trams, driven by university students enjoying their voluntary task as an exciting adventure, were half-empty, while the pavements were crowded with office-girls, shop-girls, clerks and message-boys, righteously walking to their work.

Without newspapers, the city was full of fears and rumours. For the first time, politics had become something important to the women and girls in the conglomeration of back-streets and the two-roomed tenements of the main roads. They were hysterical when they talked of the Strike, loud-voiced in a determination to support it to the end, proclaiming that at last there was an open fight between the callous rich and the long-suffering poor.

'Class against class, that's what it is,' said Mrs Houston to Mrs Higney. 'Those communist fellows are not so very far wrong when you think of it. It's up to us to stick together.'

'Aye, with traitors like Bulloch in this very street,' scoffed Mrs Higney. 'And the Lord knows what's happening elsewhere! Ach, what's the use? It'll all come to nothing, and we won't be one bit better off, you'll see! So long as there's men like Bulloch....'

'What does one man matter?' demanded Mrs Houston.

'How do we know how many more there are?' retorted Mrs Higney.

All over the city the housewives of the tenements jabbered belligerently, while their menfolk stood at the street-corners sullen and afraid. But when the first excitement faded and a housewife here and there began to wonder if the Strike was a wise thing, the husband briefly scorned her nagging worries about his job and the children and food. Determination fluctuated. The same worker would speak of the Strike in the evening as a fight that was bound to end in a quick success, and see it in the morning as a foolish struggle that would break down in total defeat. Every day it was declared that one trade union or another had decided to call its members to return to work, and every day it was rumoured that the Army were to be called out to patrol the streets.

Amid the succession of transient rumours, there came
one that persisted with a vague authentication, asserting
that a student driving a tram had been stopped by a gang
of pickets and assaulted, and then when he was running
away someone had thrown a stone at him, hitting him on
the head. The student had fallen on the cobble-stones and
died from a fractured skull. The wives of the strikers
heard of it with a grim satisfaction.

'Serves them right for interfering in something they
don't understand,' they said; 'something they know
nothing about. This is a fight. And they try to make a joke
of it. Maybe that'll learn the others!'

'Them and their plus-fours,' jeered Mrs Houston.
'They needn't try to come out to us again on a Charities
Day!'

But Mr Bulloch, portly in his green uniform and fur
gloves, went on driving a tram, with a student as his
conductor. They worked the Kelvinside to Parkhead route
together, the student joyful and garrulous and Mr Bulloch
silent and uncertain of what would happen next. It was
all right in the west-end, going along the Great Western
Road, but once they had left the centre of the city and
turned eastward he was afraid. The only thing that kept
him going was his belief that the Strike would be over in
a couple of days, and that those who were booing him
would lose their jobs for good then.

On the fourth day of the Strike Mr Hannah, secretary
of the local branch of the Transport Workers' Union,
decided it was time to attend to him. He had already
stopped a handful of doubtful cases, and the case of Mr
Bulloch was to him like a blot on his own honour. With
two lieutenants, Mr Todd and Mr Porter, he called at the
Bullochs' house in the evening, when he knew that Mr
Bulloch was off duty.

He rang the door-bell imperiously, and, gesturing to
the others to imitate his example, he straightened himself

to his full height and put on a stern expression. He was a small man, slightly knock-kneed. Mrs Bulloch opened the door a little and went red in the face when she saw him.

'We want to see your man,' said Mr Hannah. 'Right now!'

'He's not in,' enunciated Mrs Bulloch with an aloof dignity, and tried to close the door.

But Mr Hannah had already got one foot over the threshold, and with a determined shove he pushed her and the door back.

'We'll soon see,' he declared, and entered the house followed silently by Mr Todd and Mr Porter.

Mr Bulloch had gone to bed after a small meal. He was finding that he could not eat, and, exhausted with the strain of the last three days, he had thought he needed a good night's rest. But he could not sleep, and when he saw the deputation come into the room he sat up panic-stricken, clutching the blankets up to his chin.

'What do you want?' he asked, and his voice emerged with an incongruous littleness from his embedded bulk. 'Who asked you to come here?'

'Nobody,' said Mr Hannah. 'We just came. We want to see you.'

'What do you want to see me for?' demanded Mr Bulloch, looking for support to his wife, who stood frightenedly at the door of the room. 'I've nothing to say to you. I want nothing to do with you!'

'Oh, but we've plenty to say to you,' responded Mr Hannah, calmly.

'You've no right to come breaking into people's house like this!' cried Mrs Bulloch, near to hysteria. 'I'll fetch the police, that's what I'll do. I'll get a policeman to you!'

'Aye, get the Army too,' jeered Mr Hannah, and bending over Mr Bulloch he jerked the blankets down to his waist. 'Come on, you scab! What've you got to say for yourself?'

Big-chested in his thick pyjama jacket, Mr Bulloch reached frantically down and tried to gather up the blankets again to cover himself, looking as if he felt indecently exposed.

'You get out of here!' he cried in a high-pitched tremor that was trying to be a frightening roar. 'Get out of here before I get up and put you out!'

'You're getting up all right,' declared Mr Hannah, pulling the blankets away from his outstretched hands and scattering them off the bed altogether. 'You're getting up and coming with us, that's what you're doing!'

'You can't order him about like that!' exclaimed Mrs Bulloch, moving determinedly forward a step and then stopping indecisively, her hand fluttering over her large bosom.

Silently, with a grim directness, Mr Todd stepped forward and grasped Mr Bulloch's ankle to haul the tram-driver half out of bed.

'Did you join our union or did you not?' he demanded.

To save himself from falling on his back, Mr Bulloch grasped the edge of the bed and got on his feet on the carpet beside it.

'What if I did?' he panted. 'You can't force me into anything, you can't keep me from my job. I've a wife and family to keep!'

'And that's why you're blacklegging other men with a wife and family, eh?' scoffed Mr Porter.

'You miserable traitor,' said Mr Todd, with cold venom. 'The whole working-class is solid in this fight, except for a few scabs like you. Well, you're chucking it, do you hear? You're chucking it!'

'I've a wife and family to keep,' repeated Mr Bulloch, looking jerkily from one to the other of them as if he were wondering which one he should throw out first and then deciding to attack none of them.

'Aye, so have we,' said Mr Porter. 'But we're not

stabbing our fellow-workers in the back like you!'

'Do you know what you're going to do?' said Mr Hannah, sticking up his small thin face aggressively into Mr Bulloch's fat and florid one. 'You're coming out with us, and we'll take you to the Labour Hall and give you a picketing job for the morrow at the depot. You'll get your badge and your instructions.'

'I'm not, I'm not going!' cried Mr Bulloch.

'Get a hold of him, boys; we'll show him!' shouted Mr Hannah.

'Here you, what are you doing? Stop that! I'll get a policeman!' screamed Mrs Bulloch, taking another two steps determinedly forward before she halted again in alarm.

Grabbing Mr Bulloch round the waist, Mr Hannah tried to force him on his back on the bed.

'Get his trousers,' he panted. 'Not his uniform, his other trousers. We'll show him!'

But he could not shift the tram-driver's enormous bulk, even when assisted by Mr Todd and Mr Porter, and, struggling amid them, Mr Bulloch cowered in terror. In despair of carrying out his intention, Mr Hannah released his grasp and pushed him contemptuously on the chest with both hands. Mr Bulloch swayed and sagged backwards against Mr Todd. As if contaminated, Mr Todd pushed him forward again, and he fell at Mr Hannah's feet in a faint.

Erect around him, the deputation gaped, and screaming for the police Mrs Bulloch ran to her husband and knelt sobbingly beside him, rubbing his cheeks.

'So help me God!' said Mr Hannah, slowly. 'A man of his size, passing out like a lassie!'

He turned irresolutely, followed by the others, and with backward glances they sidled to the door.

'Murderers! slum hooligans!' screamed Mrs Bulloch. 'Oh, Andrew, Andrew! are you all right? Andrew, speak to me! I'll get you for this, Hannah! I'll make a police case out of it, I'll charge you! I'll get you; you wait. Bullies and ruffians! Oh, Andrew, are you all right?'

'Ach, shut your face!' retorted Mr Hannah. 'There's nothing up with the yellow-livered scab. Maybe you'd better keep him away from the depot now, or he might get worse.'

'Here, boys, get his uniform!' said Mr Todd. 'That'll keep him in!'

Hastening back into the room, they gathered up his uniform between them and marched out, their heads high, their conscience clear, and their faces slightly red.

The next morning the story of the assault and Mr Bulloch's collapse was all over the street.

'They put the fear of death in him,' said Mrs Houston, exultantly. 'He'll keep to his bed now, the scab! No more blacklegging for him for a while!'

But there was nothing more for Mr Bulloch at any time. He died in a fortnight. The doctor said it was heart trouble, and, callously scoffing, the gossips said it was just a weak heart. By that time the Strike was over, political uninterest had fallen again on the briefly disturbed city, and the only ones vocal were those saying: 'I told you so!' When the city's newspapers refused to take back the compositors who had joined the Strike, the once belligerent workers asserted to each other in gloomy agreement: 'We should never have done it. We should have made sure of our jobs first. I knew this would happen. They just made a fool of us. Leaders be damned! What do they care about the working-class? It's up to us to look after ourselves. Jobs aren't so easy come by these days.'

In the city's returned pessimism, amid the job-worrying of the tenements, the two Bulloch boys left the high school and went to work to keep their widowed mother. One became a van-boy and the other a public-house waiter.

Massive in her grief, alien to her neighbours in a bitter loneliness, Mrs Bulloch looked a meaningless megalith. She saw her sons grow up into rough-spoken young men who dressed like corner-boys and worked irregularly at blind-alley jobs. She strove to rule them and guide them, worrying about their future for them, and her ladylike voice chiding her fatherless family to its old pretence of breeding moved irrelevantly over a shattered security.

Mr Plottel's Benefit Concert

In the dim kitchen, where a fire of dross and potato peelings sullenly smouldered, Plottel stood listening to his father's monologue. The autumn rain fell steadily on the dirty water of the Canal beyond the tenement's backcourt and the city was filled with the cold odour of mud and poverty, but in the nostrils of the silent boy the smell of autumn was driven out by the smell of his father's cigarette and the lurking odour of boot-polish. Those were the aroma of his father, pervading the Sunday afternoon and containing within themselves the essence of all the occasions in which from infancy he had been conscripted to listen to his father's complaints.

'Two and ten that steak-pie cost me,' said Mr Plottel, letting a cigarette burn away between his lips as he polished his boots. 'Two and six for the pie and fourpence for the ashet. As if they couldn't trust you to bring it back. I don't want your ashet, I said. It's no use to me. What would I be doing with an ashet? I'll bring your bloody ashet back, I said. But no! She wouldn't hear tell of it, the bitch. Two and six for the pie and fourpence for the ashet. Two and ten that I could ill afford. And not a bloody word of thanks for it.'

In the front room that looked down three storeys on to the main road, Mrs Plottel lay asleep, her face covered by the *News of the World*, while the rest of her family sprawled around her, content to leave their father alone in the kitchen with his favourite son.

'Things has never been as bad as they are today,' said Mr Plottel. 'Your poor old father's up against it this time and no mistake. I've never been so hard put to it to earn a few bob as I've been this last four or five month. And the winter's nearly here. Where I'm to get a new coat from, God alone knows. There's only thing to do. I don't like to have to do it. It isn't long enough since I had the last one. But things is bad. I'll have to run another Benefit. Harry Kinsley would do the printing cheap. All you want is three or four display-bills and say a thousand hand-bills. Eight or nine turns would be enough. That's the trouble, you know. Getting the artistes. Aye, there's the rub!'

He rubbed his toecap with a soft cloth.

'You can't get them nowadays. There was a time when your old father could have called on the cream of the profession, and they'd have done anything for him. Aye, and for nothing too. But times is changed, and not for the better. There's not the same fellowship nowadays, and damn little talent either. The same old Scotch tenors singing the same old songs. A good character comedian like your father is a thing of the past, nearly. And they all want too much. As if I were running a Concert for their benefit. I run these things for Jack Ray's benefit. He's the boy that needs the money. Not these small-timers that would sell their own mother to the rag and bone man for the chance to get on a good bill.'

When he went out for the evening his family swooped into the kitchen like a tribe returning to its abode after an evil spirit had been exorcised, and Mrs Plottel asked Peter what his father had said. He delivered his report without comment, aware that in his parents' estrangement he was the necessary intermediary between them, the neutral state that served as communication between two warring powers.

'Whatever will he think of next!' cried Mrs Plottel. 'The man lives in the past. Does he really think people will pay to get into his concerts when they've got the pictures to go to? And what did he ever make out of one at the best of times anyway? Holy Mother of God, will he never learn sense? No, I suppose he'll see himself as Jack Ray, Character Comedian, to his dying day.'

In the week that followed, Mr Plottel spent his days and nights at Lauder's Corner, where the unemployed vaudeville actors of Glasgow gathered together to talk of past glories and future hopes. He found them as full of excuses as the guests in the parable of the Great Supper. To cast the pearls of their repertoire before the swine of a Sunday Evening Concert, just for the sake of a few shillings, while he took all that was left after paying expenses, was bad business to them. Some laughed him off in hostile derision, some fobbed him off with a vague mumble, some kept him warm with a promise wrapped in a cloak of threadbare reservations, and some just looked at him and said nothing. By the end of the week he hadn't a turn fixed, and on the Sunday afternoon his son had to listen to another plaintive monologue about the ungratefulness of his fellow-artistes, none of whom would ever have seen the professional stage if he hadn't discovered them and encouraged them, coached them and reared them.

'Listen, my boy,' he said abruptly after a pause and a sigh. 'I want you to help me. I want you to write a song for me, or just parody any old song that everybody knows. Make a good burlesque of it. You do that before the Concert, and if I can use it I'll give you a shilling for it.'

For another week he continued to plead at Lauder's Corner, and tramped all round the city following up the flimsiest rumours of willing turns. Ten days before the Concert he came proudly home with the printed bills. In the kitchen, alone with Peter, he unrolled one of the large posters and the boy saw a bold display of black and red lettering, loudly announcing: JACK RAY'S GRAND BENEFIT CONCERT.

He read the names and knew them all, from his father at the top of the bill to Sandy McCulloch at the bottom, in the middle a sprinkling of amateurs recently fallen within the orbit of his father from the uncharted spaces around him that harboured many a would-be star. Their painted faces haunted his uneasy sleep, making a vaudeville of his recurrent nightmares.

'One for Geoghegan's window,' said Mr Plottel, counting off the posters. 'One for Coynihan's. One for the Tibbetts' paper-shop, and one for the pub next the Masonic Halls. You fellows can start giving out the hand-bills tomorrow night.'

He called in James and John from the front room to join Peter, and divided the hand-bills equally amongst them, allotting them each a zone. The hand-bills were small, containing the same information as the posters, printed in coarse type on thin, grey paper. So after school hours Peter, James and John gave out the word of their father in the wilderness of the tenements. John disposed of his copies of the evangel sooner than the others, for he unscrupulously thrust half-a-dozen bills at a time into each letter-box on the ground floor of the blocks assigned him.

'It'll do them for toilet-paper,' he said to James, cynical of everything appertaining to his father.

On the Sunday of the Concert it rained all morning, but by twelve o'clock the raindrops were falling weakly as if tired of their task, and the afternoon was dry and mild. Mr Plottel's mood, morose in the morning, cleared with the sky, and by teatime he was happily singing old music-hall ballads, convinced that the weather had improved solely for his benefit. Provisions for his artistes were carried out to the Masonic Halls by the Three

Apostles, who went on ahead of their father after tea. Peter carried a crate of twelve bottles of beer, James carried two dozen cakes on a shallow tray covered with brown paper, and John carried a half-bottle of whisky and a half-bottle of port. The goods were obtained on credit, and intended to create for the artistes an air of hospitality, so that those who received a fee would not grumble at its smallness, and those who didn't receive one would not feel entirely unrewarded.

Mr Plottel benevolently told his sons that in return for their errand they could stay and see the Concert, but behind his back James and John derided the invitation, and when they reached the Masonic Halls they stowed their precious burdens away in a committee-room as directed, and then slipped away, leaving Peter on guard.

'Where are the other two?' demanded Mr Plottel crossly when he arrived and found Peter alone in the empty hall.

'They went away,' answered the boy timidly, with a vague idea that if he whispered the words they would not provoke so much anger as a louder utterance.

'And who told them they could go away?' shouted Mr Plottel. 'I distinctly told them to stay here. I need two of you at the door to watch the plate. I'll get some obedience in my family or I'll know the reason why.'

He paused, fuming, and his son waited silently.

'Put the plate out for the silver collection,' said Mr Plottel. 'You'll have to watch it by yourself. I've a lot to do. Put it on the table just inside the front door, and don't leave it till I tell you. And here! Put these on the plate. The public are sheep. Kid them along a bit.'

He gave Peter a florin and two separate shillings as a start for the silver collection and an example to the contributors.

'And straighten your tie,' he added. 'Try and look respectable. God, I'll never train you! Now remember, nobody gets in without putting something on the plate.'

The boy went to the front door and took his station in accordance with instructions, fidgeting with his tie and combing his hair nervously with his fingers. Shortly after seven o'clock the first trickle seeped through the doorway from the cold gaslit street outside, and before the half-hour there was a steady stream. Stout matrons with a train of children, their lean husbands tagging along in their Sunday suit and a clay pipe, courting couples with a patronising smile intended to indicate they were coming in only because there was nowhere else to go on a Sunday night, and noisy gangs of swaggering youths—they came in swarming. Yet when he looked into the hall they seemed lost in the bare expanse of it, scattered sparsely along the wooden benches.

The concert started ten minutes behind time, and from the door he heard the showman's voice of his father bellow the flattering preliminaries for the first turn. Then he heard an agonised rendering of 'On With the Motley.' Stuck at his post without relief, faithfully guarding the plate to exact due tribute from latecomers, he heard fragments of the next turns and irregular laughter at obscure jokes. Only when the concert was nearly half over was he told to bring the plate back-stage, and in a side-room he had reserved for his own use his father quickly counted the takings, grimaced at the total, and locked the money away.

Followed by his son Mr Plottel went along a dim corridor to the committee-room where the artistes gathered for the refreshments, but the boy was lost in the jabbering throng of actors, actresses and deadheads, and wandered out to the front as the sister-act danced off and Mooney and Rooney pranced on. They sang a song about girls.

'That reminds me,' said Rooney with elegant condescension, 'I met your sister last night. She's getting very fat, isn't she? Tell me, what does she weigh now?'

'Sausages,' answered Mooney.

The audience booed.

'They don't like that one,' commented Mooney impartially.

'No, it needs a shave!' shouted a youth from a gang in the front row.

'So do you,' retorted Mooney, looking down in him from the edge of the small platform that served as a stage.

His riposte was received with jeers and catcalls, and someone threw a piece of orange peel at him but missed. He picked it up and slung it casually back at the audience, where it landed on the lap of a fat woman who was sitting feeding herself from a poke of black-striped balls, and as she indignantly threw it back at Mooney the hall rose in an uproar. Mr Plottel came hurrying on with outflung arms and a powerful shout, and under his influence the hall subsided through diminishing spasms to complete order.

'See, I told you we'd be a riot here,' said Mooney calmly in the middle of the hush.

'Yes, but we don't want that kind of riot,' said Mr Plottel.

'Well, they're awfully disbelieving,' said Mooney plaintively. 'I was just saying my sister works in a butcher's. She sells sausages. You should try them sometime. Do you like a sausage for your breakfast?'

'Well, I never saw such a man!' said Mr Plottel courageously. 'But what about the show? The show must go on, you know.'

'I tell you what I'll do,' said Mooney. 'I'll sing a wee song.'

He stepped to the edge of the platform and blandly announced:

'My next number will be an old song entitled 'She Married the Village Squire because she liked his Manor":'

Mr Plottel deftly retreated, and wandering back to the committee-room when Mooney and Rooney were under way again, Peter found his father mopping his brow and looking for sympathy.

'That young ass Rooney!' he raved. 'Stands there dumb, with the place in pandemonium. He'll never learn the business! I had to go on there myself and gag Mooney along to get the show started again, and Rooney stands by with his mouth hanging open. Oh, these part-time professionals!'

Towards the end of the programme he returned to the stage, and in a speech of familiar humour thanked his benefactors for their kind and generous support of an old actor devoted solely to their entertainment. He bowed himself off to change for his act, leaving Ronaldo with his accordion to divert the audience, and reappeared in five minutes wearing a ginger wig, an Eton collar with a bow tie, a skimpy jacket, and trousers that were too long to be short and too short to be long. Standing at the side of the hall again, the boy watched the antics of his painted and powdered father, listened patiently to the comic stories with puns embedded in them like currants in a stale bun. He had heard them all before. He waited to hear the burlesque song he had written, a lugubrious ballad of domestic strife. It came at the end of the jokes, and to a tune that lurched around 'The Wearing o' the Green' his father droned in deep melancholy.

'Now this is how it came to pass, as I can well recall,
It was a foggy Friday night and snow began to fall.
My old Dad came home fighting drunk, my Mum began
    to wail,
And when he started bashing her she crowned him with
    a pail.

So Dad he threw it back at her and then he gave her
    more,
Until she slipped and cracked her skull against the
    kitchen door.
She lay there stiff, she never rose, she lay there cold and
    dead,
And Father took his hooker off and scratched his baldy
    head.

Scratching his ginger wig, Mr Plottel acted the surprise
and dismay of his fictitious father, and continued
pathetically:

'They had him up for murder and they sentenced him
    to die,
And my old Dad sobered up at last and started for to
    cry.
But they took him out and hanged him when the snow
    was on the ground
And gathered at the prison gates us poor kids stood
    around.
We grew up poor and ignorant, we never had no
    chance,
But I earns an honest copper by my humble song and
    dance.'

On the last word of the ballad Mr Plottel began a slow
tap-dance that speeded up as Mr Hitchman at the piano
syncopated the melody of 'The Battle of the Boyne,' until
in a few seconds he was dancing frantically to keep up
with the music, interspersing acrobatics with his
tap-dancing, leaping and bounding and turning
somersaults, kicking his heels together and chasing after
the music, which seemed always on the point of shaking
him off and leaving him far behind. Then Mr Hitchman

brought both hands down on the centre of the keyboard in a shattering discord. Mr Plottel got there just in time, his right foot and torso forward, his left leg flung behind him, his arms stretched sideways. His position was one of unstable equilibrium, and he appeared to be in imminent danger of falling over the edge of the stage, but with an agile recovery he leapt in the air and came lightly down, his feet together, his hands by his side, and bowed to his audience. They applauded him loudly and lengthily, the gangs whistling shrilly, and he took another bow, but the boy at the side of the hall felt that the applause was for his father's energetic display of tap-dancing and acrobatics rather than for the comic song, and the pride of authorship faded within him to a resigned boredom.

He wandered back-stage again. In the small dressingroom his father was getting rid of his make-up and changing back to his ancient dinner-suit. The boy drifted shyly to a corner, fiddled with the orange-coloured tin of Leroza's face-cream and wondered if he should mention the shilling. Ignoring his son, Mr Plottel returned to the committee-room where the artistes and deadheads were assembled. The tea was finished, the beer was gone, the whisky and port were done, and the table was littered with empty cups and glasses and the crumbs of the vanished cakes.

Outside, Ronaldo occupied the stage again and the sound of his accordion slipped unheeded into the babbling committee-room as he brought the concert melodiously to its end. Slowly the hall thinned, and when Mr Hitchman played 'God Save the King' the people who had remained to get the last dregs of entertainment for their threepenny-bit stood limply up and in a few moments they were shuffling to the bottleneck of the door, eddying out into the dark night.

In the committee-room Mr Plottel was paying his artistes, moving genially amongst them and slipping them their fee so quietly that they hardly knew they had been paid and no one saw what another received. When they realised there was nothing more to come and nothing more to drink, they made their exit with the effusive cordiality of music-hall performers, and Mr Plottel bade them good-night with a warmth no less than theirs. The doorway vibrated with loud voices calling farewells, repeating and returning compliments, so that the room seemed brimming over with good-fellowship.

The air oscillated as father and son were left alone, and came to rest in silence. Mr Plottel took a little notebook from inside the jacket of his dinner-suit and scribbled swiftly with an audible running commentary, calculating his expenses and counting the takings again.

'One pound two and thruppence profit,' he said bitterly, and sighed heavily through his nose. 'It's not worth the bloody trouble.'

The boy opened his mouth to ask for his shilling to be included in the expenses, but closed it again in fear of his father's unpredictable temper.

'Come on, it's time we weren't here,' said Mr Plottel. 'Get those empty beer bottles together in that crate. There's a penny on each of them. Take them in to Flanagan's tomorrow night, but don't say I sent you. He didn't charge me for the bottles, but we might manage to get the refund on them. He won't know you. That would be another shilling.'

He gave Peter his overcoat to hold for him while he backed into it, avoiding the torn lining of the sleeves with the automatic skill of habit, thrust the whisky bottle into one pocket and the port bottle into the other, leaving Peter to carry the crate of empty beer bottles, with the pastrycook's tray on top. Father and son walked in silence along the valley of the tall, sombre tenements, and before they reached home the boy's arms were aching with their burden. As they entered the gaslit close, his father suddenly spoke.

'You don't need to tell anybody how much we took.'

'No,' said Peter.

'I'll never hear the end of it if your mother finds out,' muttered his father, and sighed bitterly again.

'Aye,' said the boy vaguely.

He parked the crate and the tray in the lobby. Through in the front room his brothers claimed him.

'Where's the cakes?' they demanded together.

'They're all gone,' said Peter.

'How many did you have?' asked James.

'I didn't have any,' he answered, so absentmindedly as he rubbed his aching arms that his voice did not convince them.

'Ach, tell that to somebody else!' jeered John, his fist raised in a gesture that was partly threatening, partly disgusted.

'I bet you had your fill all right,' said James with a grin that was more a sneer.

'Look,' he said angrily, 'you two walked off and left me to carry all those screwtops back by myself. Suppose there had been any cakes left, how was I to carry them?'

'I knew it, I told you!' cried John to James. 'There were some cakes left over and he was too lazy to bring them. He ate them himself!'

'Oh shut up!' he shouted impatiently.

He went through to the kitchen, where his mother, hoping to share in the proceeds of the Concert, was amiably preparing supper for his father. The atmosphere was mild and held out the promise of a resumption of diplomatic relations between his parents. But he knew his mother would get nothing out of the Concert, and he knew he would never get the shilling for his song. Putting aside his fear of his father for a moment, he wondered if he dared keep the shilling on the empty beer bottles.

Onlookers

Before the newlyweds moved in, the single apartment looking on to the main road was occupied by a man and his wife
who fought every night. Regularly, just after midnight, the
woman's screeching harangue was heard rising above the
deep growling of her husband, and their only child squalled
in unheeded terror. The whole block lay wakened in darkness, waiting the climax. After the rumble of overturned
furniture came the sharp report of hurtled crockery breaking against the wall, and then the woman's loud wails. The
neighbours lived in expectation of murder, and with hetero-
sexual sympathy the gossiping wives blamed the woman for
provoking the poor man and not knowing when to hold her
tongue. Unfriended and unregretted, the quarrelsome couple moved after four months, and the tenement looked
forward to peace at midnight again and sleep unbroken by
the noise of battle going on till two and three o'clock in the
morning.

The newcomers were different. The neighbours were
sure they would never quarrel outrageously, for Mrs
Gannaway and her husband were clearly suited to each
other, agreeably placid in temperament. And Mr
Gannaway had a small tobacconist and newsagent's shop,
on the same side of the street as his house. Because of his
attentiveness, it was always busy, steadily gaining trade
from the muddled stores kept by slovenly old women in

the district. So his wife would never need to quarrel with him about money, as her predecessor in the single apartment had done with her husband, a man who had never worked.

The tenement returned to tranquillity then, and although Mrs Gannaway did not gossip with the neighbours and had no confidant among them, they had nothing against her. They saw her as a slow-moving, dreamy young woman, who smiled readily with a vague friendliness. And from the cut and cloth and number of her husband's suits, as well as from the changes in costume she had herself, they considered the newlyweds were quietly prosperous, free from the worry over money which obsessed everyone else in the tenement.

But slowly the matrons began to see something more than a leisurely content in Mrs Gannaway's slow walk and more than the happiness of an unworried bride in her bright colour. Mrs Higney declared that the young wife was consumptive, and before long all the wives in the block were taking her guess as a statement of fact, a statement made years ago by somebody, long forgotten, who had known it as a certainty. Within the year, Mrs Higney was proved correct. After a doctor had visited her for a month, Mrs Gannaway went to Ruchill Hospital, across on the north bank of the canal, to the sanatorium there for consumptives.

Mr Gannaway stayed on in the single apartment alone, attended more industriously than ever to his shop, and greeted his neighbours with brief politeness. His small business went on improving, and he increased its stock, throwing into contempt the paltry holdings of the old wives who had kept similar shops in the district long before him. Walking the few hundred yards from his shop to his home, he had the air of a man who knows he is doing well because he deserves to. His greetings to the neighbours he passed had in them something of tolerance for the shiftless and condescension to the unsuccessful, and he never mentioned his wife. As a result, the women on his own side of the street were not quite sure if they liked him or not; they were not quite sure if he were callous and secretive, or just naturally a man of few words.

But before she had been much longer than a month away, Mrs Gannaway came back from the sanatorium and slept alone every night on a long couch placed against the window, which was opened wide at top and bottom. And she rested. She rested all day. Peeping discreetly behind their curtains, the housewives on the other side of the street watched her and her husband at the window of the single apartment, and discussed with each other all they saw, alluding to it casually as if they had seen it just by accident.

Then at night, the tenement was again kept awake by a disturbance in the single apartment, less violent than it had suffered from the quarrelling of the couple who had previously lived there, and with none of its screaming terror. But it had a horror all its own, and aroused the neighbours more intermittently. It was the sound of the young wife coughing, and the way it seemed to choke and rack her made them shudder and turn round with the blankets pulled over their ears. Sometimes, when she was at her worst, she had barely time to recover her breath from one attack before she was in the grip of another, coughing harshly all through the night. And once they were sure she was as good as dead. A fit of coughing at three o'clock in the morning faded away in an exhausted rattling in her throat, and in the little brick boxes around and across from her the tenement-dwellers stared unsleepingly into darkness, waiting and wondering. But then they heard another spasm seize her, showing by its vigour that she was still very much alive. Some nights they heard an especially lengthy paroxysm end in a long low moaning, as if she were weeping.

'That's terrible!' muttered Mrs Higney. 'You'd think it was tearing her inside right out, the way it comes. She'll kill herself some night, coughing like that.'

And the woman in the little dairy down the street, which opened at six o'clock in the morning and served the early-rising matrons with rolls and milk, began to ask regularly, as a ritual greeting to her customers, 'Did you hear her last night? I think she's getting worse.'

'There was once I thought she had burst something,' the customer would answer. 'It seemed to be sort of wrenching her apart.'

'That cough alone,' said the dairywoman, 'would be enough to kill anybody. It's something awful.'

But as if to confute their pessimism and reject their robust sympathy, Mrs Gannaway began to get better. She coughed less often at night, and she began to get up oftener and go out for a walk. For nearly three months she seemed to improve, and the neighbours were almost forgetting she had ever been ill. Then, as if just idling for a few days, she returned to her couch alongside the window and lay there unmoving. She began to cough again at night, with fiercely concentrated attacks that left her gasping. But the neighbours had heard worse from her before, and insensitive to it by custom, they heard it drowsily only as a minor spasm and fell unworriedly asleep. And while they slept, Mrs Gannaway coughed despairingly on, coughed as if she were fighting to suppress it, with something apologetic in it all, until the attack won out in its full deathful insistence and left her helplessly panting in exhaustion, her head lolling over the edge of the couch.

Three weeks after she took to her bed again, early in a morning of April when the clear spring sunlight slanted over the tall tenements of the main road and made its tram-railed broadness seem clean and joyous, she died at the window while her husband, risen from his bed in the other corner of the room, sat on a chair beside her, chafing her hands in a panic.

'She's dead,' said the dairywoman to her first customer at six o'clock, so impatient to tell the news that she could not wait to hear the customer's order.

The stout, slippered matron who had come in for a dozen rolls and a pint of milk gaped in disbelief as she had seen film actresses do, and slowly said, 'But I thought she was getting better.'

'You should have heard her last night, just before she died,' said the dairywoman, nodding her head wisely to hint at all her customer had missed. And to every customer who came in that morning she said at once, 'Did you hear Mrs Gannaway was dead?' And every customer gaped a while and then slowly said, 'But I thought she was getting better.'

The funeral took place the following afternoon, and three deep against the kerb on both sides of the street the neighbours stood impatiently waiting for the coffin to be brought down to the hearse.

'There's nearly as big a crowd here as there was the time they buried the man Reid,' said Mrs Higney, looking round approvingly. 'You remember he cut his throat.'

With increasing boldness the matrons on the Gannaways' side of the street discussed Mr Gannaway with whispering hostility, their heads nodding in agreement as they listened to each other.

'If he had only cared to spend some money on her,' said Mrs Higney in low-voiced righteousness. 'God knows he could afford to. It's a wee Klondyke, that shop of his. But damn the ha'penny he ever spent to try and help the poor girl.'

'Imagine keeping her there in a single apartment,' whispered Mrs Farquhar. 'How did he ever expect any woman to get better in that place? Why, she hadn't even room to move!'

'He could easy have got her a better house than that,' said Mrs Stevenson, supportingly. 'A single apartment, on the money he's making in that shop! Just shows you how some folks'll put up with anything to save a shilling or two.'

'Aye, as long as they're all right,' said Mrs Higney. 'And damn the rest! And she came back from the sanatorium, where she might have stayed in comfort, just to do her duty as a wife. Fine way he showed his appreciation, letting her stick in that pokey wee place!'

'Even the other side of the street would have been better,' said Mrs Martin. 'We just get the sun for a couple of hours in the morning. They get it all the rest of the time over there.'

'The other side of the street!' cried Mrs Higney contemptuously. 'He could have got her a place in the country. But he never had a thought for that poor girl. All he could think of was his shop, his shop, all the time.'

'He was always running back there,' said Mrs Farquhar. 'He couldn't stay at home in peace with his wife. Afraid he'd miss a penny or two, maybe. Some husband he was, leaving her alone like that.'

'What kind of a life had she?' demanded Mrs Stevenson. 'Cooped up there in a single-end all day, with nobody to keep her company or give her a helping hand.'

'And he was never up nor down about it,' said Mrs Martin. 'Always the same smug smile when he passed you. Too sweet to be wholesome. And her there, hardly fit to raise a hand. She'd have been better staying in the sanatorium away from him, for all the attention she got when she was trying to do her best for him.'

'You'd never have thought his wife lay dying, to look at him,' said Mrs Farquhar. 'But that poor girl knew it. You could see she knew it.'

Over on the other side of the street, the matrons who,

peeping behind their curtains, had watched the Gannaways at the window of the single apartment across from them, stood silently waiting. Then slowly, like the ripples in water caused by a thrown stone, talk moved among them in whispers.

'I'm sorry for that poor man,' said Mrs Houston. 'He must have had a terrible life with her. I've seen him at that window washing dishes.'

'Washing dishes!' cried Mrs Lennie. 'He did all the cooking and cleaning in that house. He even sewed on his own buttons.'

'She sat there all day doing nothing,' said Mrs Buchanan. 'Surely she could have done some wee thing for the man. But not a hand's turn did she ever do. She'd have been better staying in the sanatorium, instead of coming back to be a hindrance.'

'Oh, it wasn't good enough for her,' said Mrs Plottel. 'She was so sure she could do it all at home. Rest, says she. Rest and fresh air, that's all the treatment they give you. So she came back and slept there with those windows wide open. Quite content to let that poor fellow look after her, when there were proper nurses for her in Ruchill. What kind of a life had he?'

'Maybe he's better without her,' said Mrs Lennie. 'She had to go, sooner or later. And she was no wife to him. A wife only in name. He did all the housework. He even served her with her meals, and she slept alone on that couch every night.'

'And all day too,' said Mrs Houston. 'He had to get his brother to look after the shop for him. He was always running up from it to attend to her. And you never saw him complain. Always put a pleasant face on it. He took it well, that man. There's not many men would have even bothered with a sick wife the way he was.'

'Well, they can't say he wasn't good to her,' said Mrs Buchanan. 'He gave her every attention. He wanted her to leave that single apartment and take a house outside the city. But not she! She said she'd miss the view on to the main road.'

'I know he was never done giving her money,' said Mrs Houston. 'Do you know, a week before she died he gave her five pounds he won on a horse. And what do you think she did? She bought herself a fine new dress. It'll do me in the summer, says she!'

'It just shows you,' said Mrs Buchanan. 'They never believe they're bad, these consumptives.... Look, there he is now!'

Bearing the front right-hand corner of the pall, Mr Gannaway came through the close. When the coffin was placed in the hearse, he turned with his brother and opened the door of the first carriage. Letting his brother enter first, he pulled out a handkerchief and blew his nose, fumbling as he did so to brush a corner of the linen over his eyes. Then, round-shouldered and head down, he went in beside his brother.

'That poor man!' whispered Mrs Houston. 'It's really better for him as it is, a young man like him, with all his life before him. And yet he feels it just the same. Did you see him wipe his eyes?'

'Did you see that?' whispered Mrs Higney. 'Wiping his eyes so as everybody can see him! Aye, it's easy to cry when it's too late. If he had only thought more about her when she was living, maybe she wouldn't be dead the day. A young woman like her, with all her life before her.'

Unemployed

Archer Street, off the main road, had once housed what the people themselves called respectable working-class families. But as the years degraded it and the new housing schemes came to make it look dirtily old, it became a slum, and its working-class changed into an unemployed class. So it was happening all over the city, and the old men, unshaven and dispirited, wore ragged suits and mufflers and their sons grew up without having ever worked. They drew their dole, idled at the corner talking of football and racing, and hoped for nothing.

In a two-roomed house at the end of the block, Mrs Chalmers lived with her son and daughter. She had been there since she was married, and passed with the tenement from stolid respectability to shabby poverty. But to her, it was simply that all the nice neighbours had gone away to the housing schemes and a lot of new common people had come in their place. Her own impoverishment she blamed on the untimely death of her husband, who had given her a wage every week for thirty years. Now at fifty-two she had to go out charring to get money. Her daughter, at twenty-eight, was earning thirty shillings a week in a confectioner's, but since the son had been idle for six years the family was always in debt, ill-dressed and joyless.

Greyhaired, sourfaced and irritable, Mrs Chalmers

rose every morning at six o'clock and went to the city to clean offices. She was usually back home about ten, and by that time Mary was gone to the confectioner's shop in New City Road where she was charge-hand. In the front room, then, the mother would find her son still in bed, and peevish to see him have the long lie she craved for her own weary limbs, she would shake him ill-temperedly and demand: 'Are you getting up at all today?'

When she left him again, the young man sidled out of the recess-bed and went through to the kitchen in old flannels and a dirty shirt. There he took his breakfast without a word to his mother. They lived sullenly together in hovering enmity. At first, when he became idle, his mother had been tolerant; but when she saw her own stop-gap job become a necessary drudgery and saw him look as if he would never work again, she worried uselessly about their future and nagged him in her worries. As the years of his idleness went on, and he was no longer getting relief money anywhere, she became so bitter against him that she did not care how she insulted him. She wanted to insult him. And dependent on her for any pocket-money he got, her son returned her hostility, humiliated at the grudging way she doled him out coppers.

But for the most part he was dulled to the penniless routine of unemployment, mooning around alone without thoughts or hopes. He did not join the other unemployed men at the street-corner, for they talked of nothing but racing and football coupons, and he hadn't even the spare sixpences that they had to put on a bet. So he kept uninterestedly away from them and their endless talk of the money they had just missed winning.

Isolated that way in his long idleness, he did little odd jobs about the house, polishing brasses, clearing the table, washing dishes and washing the windows. Sometimes he even washed the floor, and then he would sullenly feel he was no longer a man but a creature unsexed. And when he took the ashbin downstairs to the midden in the back court he was afraid the neighbours would see him and call him 'Jessie.' But he kept on doing those domestic tasks to keep his mother quiet.

Sometimes, to get away from her, he went out and roamed round the city. Then he came back so footsore and tired that all he wanted to do was lie down, and that made her gibe at him again.

'I wonder what you'd be like if you had a day's work to do,' she would mutter, deliberately fussing round the room so that he seemed to be in her way as he sprawled there in idleness.

'For God's sake, will you stop narking?' he would cry. 'Is it my fault I haven't a job?'

'Oh, just you keep on resting, you're doing fine!' his mother usually replied, trying to release her antagonism by heavy sarcasm. 'I'll keep you in cigarettes!'

'Aye, you keep me in luxury maybe,' he would sneer back at her.

One morning when she came home at ten o'clock from cleaning offices, she felt more despairingly ill-tempered than ever. The accumulated debts that her regular instalments could not overtake, and the need for a new coat for Mary, involving more debt, worried her to a fidgety anger at everything. She could not see what to do, and yet she felt they must do something, anything so long as they made an effort. So when she shook her son out of his late sleep, she was more than usually vicious about it, and feeling a vindictive insistence in the way she roused him, her son jabbed his elbow up at her and turned over.

'Come on, you! get up!' she said sharply. 'Do you know what time it is? You'll be lying there all day next. Some folk have been up since six and been out working, and all you can do is lie in your lazy bed.'

'Do you need to shake the arm off me just because you

want me up?' he demanded over his shoulder. 'What the hell is there to get up for anyway?'

'Nothing, nothing at all,' she retorted. 'Just you lie on and let two women keep you. I'll go on working till I'm sixty just to keep you, and you can go on sleeping.'

He lay on for spite, and it was nearly noon when he rose, unrefreshed by a sleep that had simply led him to another empty day. Unwashed and unshaven, he set about making his breakfast, and with growing ill-temper he found his mother get always in his way, as if she were trying it.

'Ach, for heaven's sake!' he muttered, obstructed by her again at the fireplace as he tried to put water from the kettle into the teapot. 'Can you not give us an inch or two to get some breakfast?'

'If you'd get up at the proper time you'd have all the room you need,' cried his mother. 'I've Mary's dinner to get ready.'

Placing a pot on the gas-ring, she added in loud hostility, 'The folk that work have got to be fed as well as you, you know.'

'A hell of a lot of feeding I get,' he said to her back, and going to the table he spread margarine thinly on a doughy roll.

'You're as well fed as them that's working,' shouted his mother, turning excitably.

'Ach, shut up!' he muttered, and staring sullenly before him as he sat at the end of the unclothed table he finished his meagre breakfast.

Sprawling on the armchair beside the empty fireplace after that, he turned over the pages of one of his sister's twopenny magazines, until his mother, still working about the range, almost tripped over his feet in a stumble that seemed deliberate.

'Keep your big feet in!' she cried, trembling slightly with nervous irritation. 'You hulking, lolling lump! Is that all you've got to do, just sit there and make yourself comfortable while other people do all the work outside and inside?'

'What do you want me to do?' he demanded, slowly drawing in his feet. 'Go out and make a job for myself?'

'You could light the fire now you're up,' she replied. 'Some sons could rise in the morning when they're idle and make themselves useful. But not you! A nice long lie in bed, and from the bed to that chair, that's your limit. By God, some folk are well-off and they don't know it.'

Unansweringly, he threw down the magazine and went to the bunker. There he took out the hatchet and forced one side off a broken box lying on top of the coals. Kneeling at the stone hearth, he began to chop the wood into little sticks, and there was a vicious force in the slow rhythm of his strokes.

His mother moved a plain chair back from the other side of the fireplace and stretched over to see how the stewing pot was getting on.

'Come on, come on,' she said peevishly. 'Are you going to be there all day? You get on my nerves, you do! I can't get room to move for you.'

'How much more room do you want?' he cried. 'I'm chopping the wood for the fire, amn't I? And that's what you wanted, isn't it?'

'Aye, that's all I want,' she jeered. 'Just you break up a few sticks. Don't overwork yourself, whatever you do!'

'For God's sake, will you stop narking!' he shouted in a fury, raising his hand against her face in a wild gesture. Looking at the hatchet he held in it, his mother drew back her grey lips in a sneer.

'Go on,' she scoffed. 'Use it! It'd be the first hand's turn ever you did.'

Redfaced at her sneer at his swinging the hatchet, when he had forgotten he was still holding it, he turned from her and bent to collect the sticks.

'Twenty-six years of age!' his mother went on, standing over him with her arms akimbo. 'And it's got to be kept by two women! There's men of your age keeping a wife and family. But you, you couldn't keep yourself in matches. You don't bring a penny into the house, all you can do is———'

Dropping the bundle of sticks he was gathering in his left hand, he rose again and confronted her angrily.

'Will you hold your bloody tongue?' he shouted.

'Away and work for your meals!' she shouted back. 'You—you———'

Stammering for words, she struck her old lined face snarling against his. Drawing back, he pushed her violently away with the palm of his left hand and she stumbled backwards and fell on the seat of the plain chair. The force of her fall overturned it, and she went sprawling to the floor alongside it. For a moment she lay there, astounded at his action, and he loomed over her, trembling with rage. Slowly she rose to her feet again, grasping the chair.

'You lazy idleonian!' she shouted. 'You good-for-nothing, lounging bloody scrounger!'

Her voice cracked in a screech, and she swung the light chair madly round so that it struck him on the hip. He darted back, and chasing him on the woman became an oathful, screaming fury. As he retreated, she stabbed him again and again with the legs of the chair until she had him cornered against the kitchen sink. Then with a yell of triumph she raised the chair high above her and made to crash it down upon his head. Cowering back from her, he swung up his hand, and the head of the hatchet he still held cut dully against the seat of the chair. Her grasp loosened by that blow, the mother swayed, and then with another thrust of the axe her son scattered the chair out of her hands. It fell to the floor and rolled over with its frame broken.

Panting, they glared at each other, and the mother tottered forward and clutched him fiercely by the collar of his shirt. Half throttling him, she tried to knock his head against the wall. But he wriggled vigorously and raised the axe again. His mother screamed, jerking her head aside in terror as she saw the blade come down upon her. But she moved the wrong way, and the side of it struck her flatly on the temple. Under that blow, hunched and panic-stricken, she clung tightly to her son.

'Let me go, let me go!' he cried, madly shaking himself to get free of her. But she would not release him, and brought to a mindless craze for force by the blow that had accidentally landed, he struck her again with the hatchet. She swayed sideways, barely clutching him then, looking up at him wailing with her eyes half closed. As she saw him raise the hatchet again, her fingers fell weakly from his throat. Then bleeding and pale, with a long low moan, she collapsed beside the chair at his feet.

He stood shaking above her, thwarted that she had fallen before there had been enough to satisfy his fury, and with one foot he jabbed her in the side, trying to rouse her to face him again.

'Get up!' he cried, his voice parched with excitement. 'I'll give you all you want. Have you had enough? Maybe you'll learn to hold your tongue now!'

He jabbed her again with his foot, but when she did not move a slow terror took the place of his wild desire to have her rise and go on fighting.

'Get up!' he repeated frightenedly. 'Get up! I didn't mean it. I tell you, I didn't mean it! Get up, there's nothing wrong with you!'

He stood for a moment looking down on her as she lay dishevelled at the base of the sink, her face hidden from him in the bend of her arm. His terror became a panic, and turning quickly he threw the hatchet in the open bunker. Then he ran into the front room and grabbed his jacket and cap and a muffler, and in another moment he was out of the house.

When Mary came in at one o'clock, opening the front door with her own key, she saw her mother bent over the kitchen sink, trying to bathe her head with a towel soaked in cold water. Hurrying over in alarm, she turned the sagging woman round and stared in horror. Her mother's face was grey, her lips were pale, and her hair was clotted with blood.

'Mother!' cried the girl, sick at the sight of the blood and the old face looking so deathly. 'What happened? What is it? Tell me, what happened to you?'

'I fell,' muttered the woman weakly. 'I felt faint. I must have fallen against that iron fender. I was making your dinner. I was at the fire. I fell. Oh, your dinner will be burnt!'

Large-eyed, staring with hypnotized disgust at the blood on her mother's head making the grey hairs look dirtily yellow, the girl felt faint herself. Then, slowly drooping, her mother collapsed in her arms.

Three weeks later, lounging at the corner of Archer Street and Maryhill Road, the unemployed men brightened hopefully when the newsboy came along with the result of the three-fifteen. One of them bought a paper and the rest gathered chatteringly round.

'Itsaboy, five to one!' they cried.

'So help me God, and I backed her every race till now,' lamented an old man with a growth of grey hair on his chin.

'Sorrento second, Slieve Donard and The Bear dead-heat for third place,' said the purchaser. 'That's my double in the bing.'

'Oh, here, do you see that!' cried a youth on the fringe of the crowd, pointing over the shoulders of the others. 'There's that fellow Chalmers' case. He's away for ile!'

'He's got six months, begod!' muttered the old unshaven man, his bloodshot eyes close against the print.

'Oh aye, the wife was telling me she heard them that morning,' said the purchaser of the paper with the offhanded pride of inside knowledge. 'She said he was crying when they got him. He came back to the house and they had to burst open the door. That was when the old wife was at the infirmary. He was trying to hide in the kitchen.'

'You see what it says there?' said the youth, trying to wriggle to the front. 'His old girl tried to tell the jailers that she fell and cracked her skull on the fender. Imagine expecting anybody to believe that!'

He looked up at his elders with a grin, proud of his scepticism.

'An agent ascribed the attack to a temporary lapse due to constant unemployment and depression,' read the old man with peering hesitancy.

'Ach, he was demented,' said the purchaser, spitting wisely. 'I heard about him. Look at it there! You see that, the doctor said he showed mental peculiarities.'

Isolating the last words, he enunciated them mockingly.

'They just mean he was mental,' he added offhandedly, and spitting again he shook out the paper to get at the middle pages. 'Let's see the night's programme at the dogs.'

A Marriage

Mrs Gregan lived contentedly in a two-roomed tenement overlooking the Canal. Poverty widened its hold on those around her, and the street came to harbour only idle men and shawled mothers, with hosts of ragged children playing in the gutter. But isolated in her own meagre independence she saw no change. She had lived there since she was married, and for her the street had still the tidy respectability she had seen in it as a bride. And when after Mass or Benediction she met any of her old neighbours who had moved to one of the new housing schemes, she briefly rejected their advice that she too should move.

'I'm all right where I am,' she declared. 'There's nothing wrong with Canal road.'

'But you come up and have a look at our place,' her friends insisted. 'You'll see the difference! We thought the same as you, till everybody started moving. And we weren't going to be left beside a lot of strangers from the slums. Then when we did move——oh, it was worth it! We've got electric light, back-garden, and kitchenette. And we've got a bathroom too!'

'I can't afford to move,' replied Mrs Gregan impatiently. 'I've only my widow's pension and the few shillings Danny earns.'

'Oh, but you could manage on that,' retorted her friends. 'There's really not much difference in the rents.

And think of the kind of neighbours you've got in Canal road now——all those Callaghans and Reillys and Murdochs and Thomsons. The old place has changed something terrible!'

'Well, I don't see it,' declared Mrs Gregan. 'I just keep myself to myself. I'm all right where I am. It's as much as I can afford. There's only Danny and myself. My house is all right. I've got to think of the future. I can't go throwing money away on things I don't need.'

Gossipping among themselves, her old friends called her mean.

'Pleading poverty as usual!' they scoffed. 'And her with a good pension and her son in a fine job, and no family to bring up. There's worse off than her can do a lot better. And her man had a good job before that accident. She's been in the Co. all her days, and never touched a dividend yet.'

Living frugally on in the changing street, unbefriended by the shawled, loud-voiced women who had come to it from the slums, Mrs Gregan gave all her attention to her only son. She loved him with a solicitude that obsessed her husbandless life, and everything she did was directed towards his comfort and the security of his future. She wanted him to get on at his work, put the other youths in the tenement to shame by his steadiness and success, and remain with her always. And as long as he seemed content with the house where he was born, she too was content.

He was a tall, broad-shouldered youth of nineteen, with a pallidly handsome face, and mothering him fussily she regulated his underwear in autumn, winter, spring and summer, planning his diet and his holidays, and buying him good suits and shirts to match them. Her fond dreams for his success in life had made her determine he would not grow up fit only for blind-alley jobs, and so she had sent him to a higher grade school when he was twelve. The neighbours thought then that she meant him to stay there till he was eighteen and then go to the University. But she took him away when he was fifteen, and for four years he had worked in the offices of a city newspaper.

'She was clever, the same woman,' said Mrs Callaghan. 'She knew just when to keep him on at school and when to take him away. He's been a long time in that job now. I wonder what he's getting.'

'Oh, he must have a good pay for his age. Better than many a grown man,' said Mrs Murdoch enviously. 'They get a rise every year in that place. My sister-in-law's niece works in it too. She told me all about him. They all call him Dan the Dandy. He's not liked at all, he's so conceited. But he's well-off, the same boy. Better than he deserves!'

'Hm, that wouldn't be hard,' responded Mrs Callaghan. 'My Peter was at school with him. Peter knew him before we ever came here. And Peter was top of the list when Gregan was nowhere.'

So, incongruously well-dressed amid the ragged idleness of the other youths in the tenement, and alien to them in his steady job, young Gregan lived under the management of his mother. But as he passed into the twenties he eased off her interference, selected his own suits and shirts and ties, and as he walked to the tramstop at the corner every morning he had an air of prosperity. His handsome face was expressionless when he passed any of the neighbours, and before his unrecognising aloofness they were sure he was getting on.

'It's not here they should be, him and his mother,' said Mrs Callaghan indignantly. 'With a job like his and the money she's got, they ought to clear out. Let them go to the new houses! Him and his la-di-da voice, putting on airs in a street like this!'

'He must be very clever,' said Mrs Reilly. 'You never see him without a book under his arm.'

'Ach, clever my eye!' said Mrs Callaghan. 'He's only a stuck-up young pup. I've heard all about him from them that works beside him. If my Peter had got staying on at school the same as him, he'd be in a good job the day too.'

On the top deck of the tram, after looking round to see if there were any pretty girls there, the youth would open his book where a tram-ticket was inserted and read gravely on. As he read, he caressed the back of the volume, and every time he turned a page he looked up with a blink and glanced hopefully about him for a girl to admire.

But his survey of the top deck of the tram was not due to loneliness. At a parish dance he had met a girl from Lambhill, and without his mother's knowledge he met her regularly after that. To her, he was a clever young man with prospects, and he talked to her of the books he read and what was wrong with them. Because he was not sure if she were good enough for him, since she had left school at fourteen and had a Glasgow accent, he kept on looking for another girl. With grave caution he deliberated about which of the many pretty girls he saw in the office or on the tram he should approach next. But he deliberated so much that he did not approach any of them. Then with an undifferentiated desire he made love clumsily to the girl he had, the only one he knew, and complacently amenable she grinned responsively to him and thought how handsome and smart he was.

At first they went only to a cinema, but soon they began to vary their picture-going with walks outside the city. In the evenings of early autumn they walked along the Canal bank to the wilderness beyond Lambhill, and lay together in the deepening twilight in a field across from the water. When the weather prevented their doing that, he was fidgety in the cinema, and outside it he had nothing to say to her. The days of his bookish talk to her were over, and since she had never paid much attention to it she did not miss it. All there was between them was an excited ministering to each other's gratification, and beyond the time and place where they could be safely alone for that, they were silent strangers.

When he went home at night, his mother scolded him for keeping late hours. To her, he was still a child, and she would have mothered him as fussily as she had always done. But with a life beyond her knowledge, a grown-up life of furtive love-making that exhausted and frightened him, he became less and less complacent under her attempts to control him. She saw him quiet and unconfiding and, unable to think he had anything to hide from her, she lived placidly silent with him in his silence. But in the face of his sullen reserve a timidity grew in her and made her clumsy in her authority, and that emboldened him in his evasion of it.

On Christmas Eve, tired of waiting for him to come in, she went to midnight Mass, and after it she met one of her old neighbours, a stout, waddling and gossipping matron.

'Oh, Mrs Gregan!' said the woman eagerly. 'Is it true that the young fellow Callaghan's getting married? You know the one I mean, about the same age as your Danny. They were saying he had to get married to a girl from Partick. You know what I mean.'

'I've heard nothing about it, Mrs Hurley,' said Mrs Gregan unsociably. 'I keep myself to myself. I haven't seen Mrs Callaghan for many a day.'

'Oh, but she stays right beside you,' said Mrs Hurley, beamingly unsnubbed. 'I thought you might have heard something. My, it's a changed street if that's the kind of thing that's happening! That would have been a terrible thing in the old days when I was there.'

'I've heard nothing about it,' repeated Mrs Gregan, anxious to get home and see if her son had returned.

'Oh, but everybody's talking about it,' said Mrs Hurley. 'It just shows you! That's the kind of neighbour

you've got in Canal road now. You should come up beside
us, Mrs Gregan. We've got electric light and a bathroom.
And there's a better class of people altogether.'

'I'm all right where I am,' said Mrs Gregan. 'I can't
afford to move.'

'I was hearing your boy was getting engaged,' said Mrs
Hurley relentlessly. 'Some girl in Lambhill, they were
saying.'

'My Danny doesn't bother with girls,' retorted Mrs
Gregan righteously. 'He's got other things to do with his
time.'

'Oh, I heard—' began Mrs Hurley.

'I don't care what you heard,' interrupted Mrs Gregan
impatiently. 'Danny doesn't know any girls to be getting
engaged to one. He's far too young. Besides, I need his
money. But he hasn't got a girl, and that's all about it.'

'Oh!' said Mrs Hurley, and looked at her old neighbour
with an apologetic smile that slowly changed into a
sceptical grin.

Going home, Mrs Gregan was worried about her son
for the first time in her life. She remembered his late hours
and his unconfiding silence, and she was afraid. He was
her son, her only child. After the sacrifices she had made
to keep him on at school, he had to keep her, not a wife.

When she got home, he was sitting before the fire
reading a detective novel, and looking at his engrossed
expression she felt at peace again. He was too young to
be thinking of marriage, and he was too good a son to be
getting engaged behind her back. He knew she needed his
money.

With lonely scorn she saw Mrs Hurley's hints proved
true at the New Year, when Peter Callaghan sullenly
married an undersized, common-faced girl whose
advanced pregnancy made her look squat, fat and ugly.
She thought proudly of her son, well-dressed and
handsome in his good job, living industriously with her

beyond such foolishness, while idle youths from over-crowded homes were getting married in haste and lounging their days away on the dole. She was so proud of her own respectability that she wished she were more friendly with the neighbours, to tell them what she thought of the Callaghans' latest disgrace. But there was no one she could talk to. She had only her son, and she took it for granted that such things were still beyond his knowledge.

One evening after the New Year she saw him leave his tea half finished and go mooning about the small kitchen. He kept looking at the clock and then he went quietly out without a word to her. In the silence he had reared between them she could not ask him if anything were wrong. She was unable to think of anything in particular that could be wrong, and blank-minded in her loneliness she sat beside the fire sewing.

Half-an-hour later she heard someone knock at her door. When she opened it, she saw the parish priest on the landing, a tall and sombre figure with a grey chin and unfriendly eyes.

'Come in, Father,' she said, flustered at the unexpected visit.

Taking off his hat, Father O'Hagan entered the kitchen, and turned to face her as she came after him.

'Is your boy Daniel in, Mrs Gregan?' he asked in the curt, tired voice for which he was notorious in the parish.

'Oh, he's just gone out, Father, just a little while ago,' she answered, looking at him wonderingly.

'He knew I was coming,' said Father O'Hagan. 'He should have been in. I told him.'

He spoke with a slight Irish accent, standing before the fire with his hands behind him and his legs wide apart.

'I don't understand, Father,' said Mrs Gregan, vaguely disturbed. 'He kept on looking at the clock, and then he went out—I thought he was going somewhere special.'

'Hm, I see,' murmured Father O'Hagan. 'Well, maybe it's as well he's not here. I don't think you know what's been happening, Mrs Gregan.'

'No, I don't, I don't know what you mean, Father,' said Mrs Gregan, twisting her fingers as she looked at the priest in alarm. 'I don't understand. There's nothing wrong, is there?'

'Well, you're a wife and a mother, Mrs Gregan,' said Father O'Hagan. 'You know the world and the temptations of the world—and the temptations of the flesh. Your boy has been going with a girl for some time now. A girl from Lambhill. Her folks came to see me. She's in trouble. I saw your son about it. He's got to put it right. That's how I found out you knew nothing about it. He said he couldn't tell you by himself. He was to be here when I came, and then we'd straighten it out together. But maybe it's as well he shirked it. We can talk frankly ourselves. And I've it all arranged anyway. They can be married quietly after Mass at the end of the month.'

As he spoke, Mrs Gregan stared up at him with her mouth hanging open. Three times she tried to interrupt him, but her mouth was dry and no words would come. When he had finished, the priest looked slowly down at her, and with a frightened swallow and a stammer at the start she hurried her words.

'But Danny's only a boy! I need Danny!' she cried, and her voice was bewildered, rising to a nervous screech as if she were going to break down and wail in tears. 'I need his money. You can't do that. You can't go marrying my boy off like that! I need him. He can't be married. He's far too young! And I need his money, I tell you. Danny——Danny can't be married! He's only a boy!'

She turned quickly from the priest with her face in her hands, and her shoulders were bent and shaking as she wept like a child.

'He was old enough to get that girl into trouble,' said

Father O'Hagan, swaying on his heels and looking at the carpet.

'I won't allow it,' said Mrs Gregan wildly, turning on him. 'It's not fair! My boy's not going to marry some worthless girl that's led him astray. I've only my widow's pension. The little I have in the bank—anything might happen to me! It's nothing! I need Danny's money. I won't allow any marriage, I won't allow it!'

'You won't stop it, as long as I'm parish priest,' said Father O'Hagan grimly. 'Come, be sensible, Mrs Gregan! You can't speak of the girl like that. If there was any leading astray in it, I've no doubt your boy did his full share.'

'But he can't afford to get married,' said Mrs Gregan weakly, her voice exhausted by her sobs and complaints. 'He's only getting a few shillings a week. They make all the difference in the world to me. But he couldn't keep a wife——he couldn't keep a wife and family on them. A pound a week! He can't be married on that!'

'A pound a week?' repeated Father O'Hagan, looking at her obliquely. 'Oh no, Mrs Gregan! Your boy's getting a lot more than that. I don't know what he's been telling you. But he's getting two pounds ten just now. I know all about that side of it. There's no difficulty there. And even if there were——'

'But he's only been giving me fifteen shillings,' said Mrs Gregan, straightening with a jerk from drying her eyes and looking at the priest as if he were cheating her. 'He kept five for himself.'

She stopped drying her eyes and wept unrestrainedly again.

'Oh, I'd have let him have more pocket-money,' she wailed. 'I'd never have kept money from him! And this is the way he's been treating me! Why couldn't he tell me?'

'When we start deceiving those nearest to us, we get into a terrible tangle of lies,' murmured Father O'Hagan, his hands behind him and his head thrown back with his eyes meditatively on the ceiling. 'But there it is!' he went on quickly, bringing his head down again as if considering there was no use wasting the theme for a sermon on a solitary listener. 'He can well afford to get married, Mrs Gregan. There's many a man on the dole keeping a wife and seven of a family on less than your boy's getting in a secure job.'

'The shame of it!' moaned Mrs Gregan, going unsteadily to the armchair beside the fire and sitting there on her sewing with her brow resting on the back of her hand. 'The disgrace! How will I ever look the Callaghans in the face? Oh, it's the grace of God his father's not alive to see this day!'

'Come, come, Mrs Gregan,' said Father O'Hagan impatiently. 'We must take the trials God sends us. You're the boy's mother. He's been foolish, he's been very foolish. But when we're going to put it right, you must help us. It's up to you to advise him now, to help him in his marriage. It's not getting such a good start that we can afford to leave him alone. We must work together, and pray for God's blessing on it.'

'I'm his mother all right,' said Mrs Gregan, looking up with a sudden fierceness. 'And a good mother I've been to that boy. I'd have given my life for him! And this is how he's been behaving!'

The expression of fierceness passed at once from her face, and she broke down and wept hysterically again, crumpled on the armchair. Then she looked up and blinked, and her face was old and bewildered in her newly-realised loneliness as she mumbled to herself: 'Why couldn't he tell me? Why didn't he tell me? If he'd only brought the girl here ... He didn't need to go and do that. They might never have been married ... There was no need for that.'

Round-shouldered in her grief, with tears trickling

down the side of her nose, she stared at the low fire.

'I didn't even know he was going with a girl,' she whispered miserably, drying her eyes with the back of her hand. 'And I thought I knew him. I thought he would have told me everything, the way I looked after him. He knows I've only got my widow's pension.'

A Rainy Day

'It's bad,' said Mr Morrison. 'And it's on for the day by the look of it.'

'Oh, I suppose so,' said Mrs Morrison. 'Look at the weather it's been for weeks! And now this, just because we were going away for the day.'

'Are we not going to go?' asked the two children in unhappy timidity together.

'We can't go in that,' said their father.

'And you're sorry,' said Mrs Morrison.

'Of course I'm sorry,' he answered, bridling. 'I promised to take you and the kids to the coast for the day, didn't I? And I always keep my promises, don't I? But you couldn't ask anybody to go in that weather.'

'There's nobody asking you to go in that weather,' retorted Mrs Morrison, well aware that he was glad for the excuse to postpone the outing he had promised them to make up for the summer holiday he could not afford.

Watching the untiring rain with relief, Mr Morrison felt duly rewarded for his generosity in thinking of giving his family a day at the coast. In letting him break a promise he had not been anxious to keep, the weather left him free to seek the male company he craved after long absence from it. He turned contentedly from the window, leaving the children pressing palms and nose against the pane in a miserable study of the cause of their disappointment.

With the morning paper spread out on the table, elbows on the board, and his jaws resting on his hands, he waited his breakfast. His wife, with plates in each hand, violently nudged him. Lifting the paper, he veered to let her set the table, and looked across at the window again to gladden himself with the sight of the steady windless rain. Its sodden and dimming chilliness was not only his desired release from a boring outing, but the memory-filled background of many a drinking-party like the one he now anticipated.

He lay on the sofa after he had eaten, reading and picking his teeth. But the weather which was comforting to him was blankly depressing to the others, and the boy and girl quarrelled in undertones, aggrieved at the collapse of their expectations but afraid of their father's uncertain temper. Mrs Morrison went resignedly about her housework and scolded in spasms of peevishness totally unrelated to the amount of noise they were making. Mr Morrison breathed heavily down his nose to give the understood sign of his breaking temper.

'Is it them or you that's making the row?' he asked. 'For God's sake, some of you hold your tongue.'

'And if I let them carry on it's a fault,' answered Mrs Morrison.

After the midday meal he sprawled again in lazing repletion on his armchair, and the soothing anticipation of the evening he planned kept him in tranquillity, his eyes unreadingly on his newspaper. In the company of his old friends, he would not have to spend much, not even his equal share. They had known him so long, and treated him with such jocular sympathy because of his early marriage and his family responsibilities, that they never let him pay for a second round. They were what he called real pals, and because they were all unmarried and better-off than he was, he laughed off their patronising generosity in order to take full advantage of it.

But he found that thinking about the evening made him restless, so that he began to look frequently at the clock. He rose for a cigarette, economically tearing a strip off his newspaper and getting a light at the kitchen-fire. Mooning around the small room, he eyed his wife furtively and tried to gauge how near she was to getting tea ready, but he was afraid to ask her. After tea, he would go out casually, as if nothing special were on. He knew where the boys would be to begin with, and he was sure he could easily time his moves so as to walk in on them as if by accident.

Relaxing to calm again after a worry that he was going to be handicapped by her tardiness, he saw his wife fill the kettle and put it on the gas-ring. As she took his box of matches from the dresser and turned to strike one for the gas, somebody knocked at the door.

'That's like Mother,' said Mrs Morrison.

'My God!' muttered Mr Morrison at the side of his mouth, distracted from complaining about her extravagance with his matches, his lips retracted in disgust. He sat heavily down and shook out his paper viciously. Patting her hair, Mrs Morrison opened the door and her mother came gushing in.

'Oh, what a day!' she cried, immediately giving her umbrella to her daughter and taking off her hat and coat.

'Aye, it's raining,' said Mr Morrison, irritated to see her uninvited haste in making herself at home. She turned to face his usual hostility with her usual contempt, but he was hidden behind his newspaper, and thwarted that he could not see the crushing look she had prepared for him, she turned to the children who came running expectantly to her. But she had nothing for them, and they retreated in hopeless discontent with the day.

'I was going to go round to Jean's,' said Mrs Campbell to her daughter, 'but it was such a miserable day, and she's so far away—'

'So you just came round her,' said Mr Morrison to his newspaper.

'Are you staying for tea?' asked Mrs Morrison.

'Well—' said her mother.

'Sure, stay for supper too,' said Mr Morrison. Disliking his mother-in-law, he was made fidgety by her arrival, afraid her fussy interference might hamper or even prevent the departure he planned to make when tea was over, and her unwelcome presence made him more anxious than ever to get out to the friends and liquor he missed as he listened to the gossip of the two women. Turning in boredom to the front page of his paper again, glancing up apprehensively at the clock his mother-in-law had given him as a wedding-present, he heard his wife say there was nothing in the house for tea. She would have to go out and get something.

'Have you nothing at all you could make do?' asked her mother. 'Any makeshift will do for me.'

'Aye, but there's more than you in the house,' he muttered.

'Oh, you were always fond of your meals,' said his mother-in-law quickly.

'If that's the case, it's something you never got the chance to find out,' he answered with equal promptness. 'You never fed me in your life.'

'And maybe you fed me?' said Mrs Campbell loudly.

'Oh, a few times,' he said, throwing his cigarette-end in the fire with a contemptuous dismissal that was more for her than for it.

'I never came much about you till Mr Campbell died,' said Mrs Campbell. 'And even at that I've never been beholden to you for my meals. Thank God I can still keep myself. And there's nobody can say Mr Campbell couldn't keep a wife. Mr Campbell could always give his family a fortnight at the coast every summer—unlike some folk.'

'Meaning who?' said Mr Morrison, wagging his head encouragingly.

'If the cap fits,' she said.

'God, and that's a good one,' he said with a heavy snort of contemptuous amusement. 'Some men could keep a wife all right if they weren't keeping her mother too.'

'And when did you ever keep me?' cried Mrs Campbell, straightening her double-chinned head and pushing out her large bosom.

'I never said I kept you,' said Mr Morrison.

'Well, what the hell are you hinting at?' demanded Mrs Campbell.

'I'm not hinting, I'm just saying,' said Mr Morrison. 'As you say, if the cap fits.'

'Oh, never mind him, Mother,' said Mrs Morrison. 'For goodness sake hold your tongue, John! You know perfectly well we don't grudge Mother the little we can give her.'

'So long as she admits she does get something,' said Mr Morrison.

'I don't admit it,' interrupted Mrs Campbell at once. 'And whatever Mary gives me has nothing to do with you.'

'Except that she gets it from me,' said Mr Morrison. 'Maybe enough for a holiday once a year.'

'If you grudge your wife's mother having tea with you once in a while,' said Mrs Campbell.

'Once in a while!' exclaimed Mr Morrison. 'I might as well be keeping you, the number of times you come here to be fed.'

'John, hold your tongue!' said Mrs Morrison in mingled anger, fear and shame.

'Oh, so you do keep me, you do say you keep me?' said Mrs Campbell in a tone strangely triumphant.

'Ach, go away and shut up!' said Mr Morrison.

'I'll not shut up just for you,' cried Mrs Campbell. 'But

I'll go. I'll go right now. I never stay where I'm not wanted.'

In impartial anger, Mrs Morrison tried to out-shout them, but too engrossed in their own words to listen even to each other, they paid no attention at all to her who was just intruding in their fight. Both loudly speaking at once, they continued their charges not only independently of her interference, but independently also of what each heard the other say, and it was only when one of them had to stop for breath that the other had the similacrum of an audience, until when breath gave out there too the temporary listener had the chance, immediately taken, to insert the continuation of shouted insults.

Mrs Morrison then gave up her attempts to derail them to peace, and standing by in unregarded bitterness she watched the scene she had often watched, provoked as always by it to anger against them both, that they so eagerly seized the slightest material to begin and prolong the quarrel that took place every time they met. When the door banged after mother's quivering exit, she slowly began to set the table.

'Ach, come on, let's have some tea,' muttered Mr Morrison as if they were co-sufferers and tea a reward they merited together. But his wife's tight-mouthed stare of antagonism came at once to dissociate her from the alliance he was trying to imply had been between them.

'You don't deserve any tea,' she said, suddenly stopping her setting of the table, taking off her apron and throwing it over a chair as if she were resigning her charge.

'She gets on my nerves,' said Mr Morrison defensively.

'It doesn't strike you that you might get on other people's?' she asked him coldly.

'Oh, I get on yours I suppose? Well, I can tell you, you get on mine!' he responded, jolted to a panic to see from the clock how long the quarrel with his mother-in-law had taken.

'There you go again,' said Mrs Morrison. 'Nobody can say a word to you but you look for a fight. You'd start a fight in an empty house, you would.'

'Cut out the arguing, and give us some tea,' cried Mr Morrison fretfully.

As if she knew his impatience was due to his anxiety to get out to company of which she disapproved, she moved with deliberate slowness, even going out to buy provisions for the tea, although her remark that she would have to do that had been a lie, socially conditioned by her mother's presence. Having already implied that he expected something to be got in for tea, and afraid of betraying his eagerness to be off, Mr Morrison dared not say that what was in the house would do, and that it was speed rather than adequacy of serving that he was wanting.

It was then much later than he had meant, when he entered the bar which was his friends' favourite rendezvous for starting off on a night's drinking, and it was with the realisation of what he had feared that he saw strangers in the corner his friends would have occupied had they been in the bar at all. There were so many places they might have gone on to, that he was confronted with a quest too extensive to be completed before closing-time. He felt cheated, and blamed his misfortune on his mother-in-law for keeping him late. After looking sourly round the bar, he beckoned the charge-hand over.

'Has Peter or any of the boys been in tonight?' he asked.

'Peter?' said the charge-hand with the suppressed embarrassment of the public servant who has affably to pretend a good memory for names and faces. But his experienced agility rescued him, and he plunged before his questioner could see he had stopped to think. 'Oh, you mean Peter! Oh yes, he was in early on for half-an-hour. With that bookie fellow, what do you call him? Frankie. They said they were going right away for the week-end.

Peter was saying they had got a couple of women.'

'Oh!' said Mr Morrison, quite unable to hide his dejection.

'You don't need that sort of thing,' said the charge-hand grinning. 'Have it right in town, eh?'

'Aye, on draught,' he said mechanically. But as he spoke, and in his disappointment, the absence of his friends was a loss more keenly felt by him than any satisfaction at the potential presence of his wife, and their brief escapades were more alluring to him than the assured company of the woman to whom he was married.

'Would you like a draught beer?' said the charge-hand.

'No, I won't bother,' he muttered, and went unhappily out, unwilling to spend money in drinking alone. Then, although he had been told that the leaders of the group were away and could not be in any bar in town, and although the members of the coterie so disintegrated were as likely to be sitting at home as anywhere else, he went with hope springing eternal to the bar his friends were next most likely to visit. There, apparently having been drinking all evening, he saw three men he knew well enough to join. In his gloomy loneliness, seeking distraction, he went over to them. But the knowledge that they would expect him to pay his fair share inhibited him from being at all responsive when they made a space for him with the loud cordiality of intoxication.

He felt he could not make up the start they had on him, and the dregs of his bad temper and his worry about how much he was spending were handicaps increasing their start. Soberly alien to their drunken happiness, he stood unsociably amidst them until the memoried atmosphere of the bar, its warm noisiness and alert waiters, its brilliant lights on bright rows of fascinating bottles, combined with the mixed liquor he had taken to induce in him the first stage of intoxication. The alluring gantries swayed to an unsteadier confusion the more he drank, mingling with the mirrored duplication of the thronged reality about and including him, but in spite of his lightheadedness he was still far from the carefree relaxation of the others.

He was then aroused by their talk, which became increasingly sexual. The rounds of circumstantial stories of easy loving followed more rapidly than the rounds of drinks, and if the barman had not called 'Time now, gentlemen, please!', Mr Morrison would have been willing to stand another round for the sake of hearing more anecdotes. He was not drunk, but the liquor he had taken had made him more impressionable than normally, and he was excited by the stories he had heard. Feeling too sober to be at ease with these men when they all went noisily out together, he lagged behind to slip away from them at a crossing, and walked home alone. He was happier than he had been, with an intention in which a moribund affection and tenderness orientated an undifferentiated sexual excitement.

When he reached home he found he had come out without a key. He knocked with a gentle quietness that was itself an unconscious toning of how he meant to approach his wife. He heard no movement and there was no answer. From the street, and from the backyard of the tenement, he saw every window dark. The rain, which had stopped as if from exhaustion in the later part of the evening, now came apologetically on again with a spasmodic wind. For the second time in one night he felt the twinging irritation of disappointment in a nurtured plan, a fidgety anger that made him swear and feel empty in the middle. He waited in the shelter of the tenement-close, broodingly smoking and scowling at the dirty mirrors of the disturbed puddles in the gutter. Slowly the affection and tenderness which had coloured his desire for his wife faded, leaving only a growing rage that she to whom he had hurried was not immediately available. The streets became more and more deserted, and the tramcars passed at increasingly longer intervals.

'God, is she never coming!' he cried out, seeing nobody near enough to hear him and releasing his thwarted energy better by the vigour of talking aloud than by muttering to himself.

It was nearly midnight when, after waiting almost two hours, he saw her come with the two children tiredly behind her. In her walk and appearance he saw again the grace and attraction he had seen in her when she was a girl. The years of marriage had not ruined her beauty, but served only to ripen it, and her tall, maternal build so pleased him that his desire for immediate possession of her, smothered by the irritation of his long wait, flared up again at once. But he had to get rid of his bad temper first.

'Where the hell have you been till this time?' he demanded as soon as she was within hearing.

'We went round to the pictures, and we met Mrs Hamilton, and then we went up to her house and had tea,' said Mrs Morrison calmly, as if his question had been calmly put to her.

'Fine bloody carry-on!' he cried. 'Keeping me waiting here till this time, standing here for more than two hours in all this rain!'

Like a policeman moving on loiterers, he gestured her to go on upstairs.

'You didn't need to stand in the rain,' she murmured unworriedly.

'When I come home I expect somebody to be in,' he carried on in the blind momentum of his temper, his irritation increased by her calm refusal to pay any attention to it.

'Well, if you're in such a hurry to get out and meet your pals that you forget your key, whose fault is that?' asked Mrs Morrison, sending the children on in front.

'It doesn't matter whether I forget my key or not!' he

cried impatiently.

'Don't shout on the stair,' said Mrs Morrison. 'At this hour.'

'Aye, at this hour,' he jumped at the opening. 'A fine bloody time to come in at!'

'I do it once in a blue moon,' said Mrs Morrison. 'And from all appearances you were going out for one of your late nights. Oh, I know!'

'It looks like it, doesn't it?' he retorted triumphantly.

'Oh, I suppose you didn't see your pals, that's all,' said his wife, unperturbed, opening the door with her own key. 'If you had, I could have stayed in Mrs Hamilton's till two in the morning and still been back here before you.'

'Oh, shut up!' he shouted, finding everything still evade his control and the futilities of the day continue on into the night. In helpless knowledge that not this way would he manage to reach her, his anger increased as he followed her into the dark and silent house, an anger against this anger that was his, reared up and brooded: he knew it was keeping him from getting the chance to lead up to and fulfil his intention with her, and yet until he released it all against her he was not free to approach her.

'Shut up yourself,' said Mrs Morrison, momentarily out of her usual calm with his fits of bad temper.

'Between you and your mother,' he began reasonlessly, with a sudden recollection.

'Keep my mother out of it,' she said. 'She may be bad. I never said she knew when to hold her tongue. But God knows you're a thousand times worse.'

She went over to the gas-jet and asked politely for his matches. He threw them to her, and at that moment the effect of his insufficient liquor seemed suddenly to leave him altogether, and he wanted another drink. He felt cold and thwarted, and standing trembling in the darkness he felt his desire for her sharpened by her armour against him. He wanted to boss her right away, and find compensation for all the disappointments of his day in rudely forcing her to obey him. The little kitchen was illumined to its familiar immobility by her putting the flaming match to the mantled jet, and in accumulated frustrations seeking physical relief, he violently jerked off his coat and threw it over a chair.

'Don't be so tidy,' said Mrs Morrison.

'Shut your bloody face, will you!' he cried, and as she made to move past him to lift his coat, she brushed against him. With an uncontrollable rage against her tranquillity, he grabbed her by the shoulders and shook her violently. When she struggled at once to free herself, he tried to draw her into him, and they wrestled halfway round the room until she stumbled against a chair and knocked it over. Warmed with excitement, he felt the power of his sexual mastery over her grow stronger within him even as her body slipped from his hands. For a moment he too lost his balance and almost fell on top of her. But as she came on her knees beside the overturned chair, he recovered himself and swayed clumsily over her, gazing stupidly down at her dishevelled panic and panting loudly. She knelt there motionless a little while, staring up at him in astounded understanding of his state. Then the forgotten children began to whimper, and she rose with an exaggerated show of dignity to stress her contemptuous forbearance, and turned unspeakingly from him to them.

The Egg

Hoddam and Donovan shared a room in the sergeants' quarters and Hoddam was going on leave. He was a country boy and he had got the eggs from his uncle's farm in the first place.

'I can get more eggs when I go home,' he said to Donovan the night before he left. 'You take these. I'm not going to carry two eggs all the way back to Devon with me.'

So Donovan took the two eggs gratefully, and in the morning he gave one to the Mess waiter to fry for him. It came back between two sausages, and what a difference it made to them! He ate it slowly and carefully, so as not to miss the savour of any of it. The next morning, it was beans on fried bread for breakfast, and he didn't bring out his egg. Patiently he took what was going, and decided to hold on to the second egg until the bacon ration came round.

Then he changed his mind. He was in love with an A.T.S. corporal who worked with him, and he thought of offering her the egg. She was a lively girl who seemed unaware of his admiration, and trying to look at her in cold blood he sometimes thought she was frivolous and conceited. But he couldn't convince himself, and he never missed a chance to follow her around, even when the job was one she could easily do by herself. It made other people talk, and the only person who didn't seem to notice he was always at her heels was the girl herself. She was friendly, very friendly; she was even affectionate in her own frivolous way, but she was never serious with him.

Her lighthearted attitude discouraged him at times, made him depressed and irritable. Even at his best, he was quick to anger, and because she was the cause of his ill-humour he spoke to her more sharply in his moodiness than ever he did to anyone else. Then she would take offence at his manner and criticise him coldly to his face. She told him he was the moodiest man she had ever met. So out of nothing there arose with tedious frequency a sharp and bitter quarrel, his hot temper fanned to a blaze by the cold wind of her critical spirit.

This happened on an average once a week, and every time it happened he was miserable. When she flounced off and would not speak to him until he apologised, he suffered all the pains of nervous indigestion, severe headaches, and acute melancholia, and knew he was in love. It was always he who had to make it up, for he could not endure waiting for her to relent. Their reconciliations were always very tender, with all the shyness of a love unavowed between them. Another spell of affectionate friendship would follow, and once again he would hope that, given the time and the place, he might approach her seriously and not be refused, so gentle she was with him in the sunny spell of their peacetime, so thoughtful, considerate, attentive and watchful, as if they were indeed lovers who kept only their kisses for privacy.

The morning he had beans for breakfast was in such a sunny spell, and it was as she worked alongside him in the forenoon that he thought of offering her the egg. She was always talking of food, and at the most unexpected times she would cry, 'Oh, I would love a plate of steak and chips right now!' Or she would murmur tenderly, 'Just imagine! Wouldn't it be lovely if we had roast chicken for dinner!'

And she would gaze into space, an enraptured look in her big brown eyes as if she saw approaching her in the distance the food she had spoken of.

When he spoke to her of the egg, she exclaimed at once, 'Oh no! I couldn't do that! Really, I couldn't! You have it yourself!'

But he saw her eyes sparkle, seeing before them the mirage of a fried egg, flanked perhaps by a rasher of bacon, and he saw he had made a mistake in asking her. As a well brought-up young lady, all she could do was politely refuse. The only thing for him to do was to bring it in to her, and make her a present of it.

So before he went on parade the next morning, he took the egg from his cupboard and put it inside his hold-all, wrapping two handkerchieves round it first as shock-absorbers. He put the package in the lefthand pocket of his greatcoat, and as he marched a party over to the Workshop from the Camp, he was conscious all the way of the precious, fragile, brittle egg in his pocket. A morbid fear possessed him of breaking it, in spite of all its wrappings, and even to think of the mess it would be in his pocket made him hot around the brow. It was with profound relief, as at a catastrophe circumvented, that he dismissed his squad and carefully hung his greatcoat in a safe corner of the shed, the egg still uncracked in his pocket.

Snow had fallen during the night, and the morning was cold, the sky clear, the air invigorating. He went about his work, happy just to be alive on such a morning. He was in no hurry to present her with the egg. Instead, he wallowed in the anticipation of how pleased she would be when he gave her it, and how bright her smile would be as she thanked him. Several opportunities came his way, but he spurned them all, awaiting the perfect one where there would be no danger of anyone coming along to interrupt the graceful presentation he planned to make.

She passed him as he was signing a driver's work-ticket, and he completed his signature with his eyes on her retreating figure instead of on the slip of paper he was resting on the bonnet of a Bedford truck.

'Fill the Morris twelve too this morning, will you, Elsie, please!' he called after her genially.

She waved in acknowledgement, a wrench in her hand, sending a smile over her shoulder to him. Even in a battledress blouse and slacks, she seemed ineffably graceful to him as she moved through her daily routine with a song on her lips.

Quarter of an hour later he came upon her again on his way to the office.

'Have you filled the Morris yet?' he asked conversationally.

'No,' she said derisively. 'I filled the Humber. That's enough.'

'But you fill the Humber every morning,' he said in dismay. 'Doris is bound to need the Humber. You don't have to be told about it. It was the Morris I asked you to fill.'

'There's no point filling the Morris on a morning like this,' she retorted.

'Look, Elsie,' he said in exasperation, his voice rising. 'When I tell you to fill the Morris, I mean the Morris. I'm not talking about the Humber.'

As he spoke, he was conscious they had an audience, although the members of it—four auxiliaries, a lance-corporal, and three privates—vaguely pretended to be engrossed in their own tasks. But he had plunged in too deeply to get out at once, and the girl's calm defiance infuriated him.

'What's the point of filling the Morris on a morning like this?' she repeated. 'It's far too cold, and I'm too busy to keep running to it to see if it's freezing or not.'

'It's not cold!' he shouted dogmatically. 'Not as cold as

that anyway. And why the hell do you think I told you to fill the Morris?'

'I don't know,' she answered airily. 'I've never pretended to fathom the workings of your mind.'

He gaped at her, hearing his audience titter behind him, and he realised in alarm that for all her calm answers she was as furious as he was, white with anger. Another quarrel was the only ending, another day wasted, another spell of misery, oppressed by her unforgiving silence, until he mustered enough humility to apologise.

'I told you to fill it,' he said patiently, trying to speak quietly, 'because I know it's going to be needed. Captain Jamieson said he would want it any time after ten.'

'Well, why don't you tell me these things?' she demanded, and walked off and left him.

He turned the other way in a temper and saw his unwanted audience grinning in appreciation of his performance.

'Get mobile!' he shouted fiercely.

After dinner he sought her out and approached her wearily, his wrath all gone. She was tight-mouthed and hostile, and when she saw him coming she tried to walk away.

'Look, Elsie,' he said, shyly restraining her. 'Why do you always have to start a fight about the simplest things?'

'I don't start any fights,' she said primly. 'You start them. You bawl me out in front of everybody as if I were a kid.'

'But damn it all, girl!' he cried. 'You just plain defied me. What did you expect me to do? Give you a medal? Why do you always try to put me in the wrong?'

'I prefer not to try to speak to you at all,' she retorted, and again she walked off and left him.

For the rest of the day she avoided him, and when she had to speak to him in the course of her work she addressed him not, as usual by his name, but coldly and formally by his rank, so that he felt a wall between them.

He carried the egg back with him in the evening and put it back in his cupboard. The next morning, he took it to the Mess with him. There was bacon for breakfast.

'Here, get this fried for me, please,' he said, thrusting the egg into the waiter's hand.

Greater Love

He picked up his pass in Company Office before tea, and after cheese pudding and bread and jam in the Mess he hurried to the station. It was only a forty-eight hours pass, and he knew he was wasting half the value of it by going on a Friday evening to come back on Sunday, for Sunday was a free day anyway, but he was sick of the usual week-end routine, the same dances, the same girls, and the same surfeit of beer ending in the same drunken revelries. A craving had grown on him, a craving for all he thought he had grown accustomed to forget. He wanted to see his wife, he wanted to see his little girl, and he wanted to sit at his own fireside, to have again a Saturday night at home out of khaki, an evening of sobriety and quiet with his pipe and the paper, away from the Camp dance, away from the noisy over-crowded bar of 'The White Swan' where he sat drinking pint after pint and standing round after round, singing bawdy songs because everyone else was singing them, spending more than half his pay in a night. The sedate domesticated dullness of his wife that had bored him on his last leave now seemed to offer precisely the happiness of mind and body that he had sought to find in the arms of girls in uniform whose gaiety and cameraderie had made his wife's virtue seem tedious in comparison. So on a sentimental impulse he had fiddled a forty-eight hours pass when he wasn't entitled to one.

The bus to the station was crowded, the station itself was crowded. He went to the lavatory, and that was crowded. When the train came in, it was crowded too. Soldiers, sailors, air-force men and A.T.S. girls got in his way everywhere. The whole world seemed to be in uniform. He was sick of the sight of khaki and air-force blue; his only aim was to get home as quickly as possible and sit across from his wife at the fire, watching her knit, while the kid played on the carpet with the doll he had sent her at Christmas. He had to stand all the way, between the pullman coaches, and just as the train was approaching the station he heard the sirens go. The overwhelming wail alarmed him momentarily just as much as it used to do in the worst nights of the blitz, and his stomach turned over.

'Ah!' said a corporal brightly, standing alongside him. 'A spot of excitement at last! I could be doing with some.'

'Oh, it will only be another nuisance raid,' said a private in the Engineers, yawning. 'Jerry's day is over—he just hasn't got it now. What do you think, sergeant?'

He was annoyed at being spoken to. His thoughts were at home, and he resented a soldier intruding on them as much as if that soldier had intruded in his home itself.

'He can still do a hell of a lot of damage,' he said abruptly. 'It's not the first bloke that has lost everything in one of these local raids. It's no consolation to him if you say,Oh it was only a nuisance raid.'

'You got something there, sarge,' said the corporal.

He grunted in uninterested acknowledgement and made no further conversation. When the train stopped, he was first out, and ran all the way to the bus. The trouble was well under way by that time, the ack-ack barrage was increasing, and flares were dropping on the north of the city. He had to wait for the bus that would take him home, and standing in darkness he chafed and swore, wishing he could have a smoke. Then he had to fight to get on the bus, and all the way it seemed to crawl, a darkened vehicle lumbering through the darkness of a night that was given over entirely to chaos and noise. The sky was filled with flashes and loud with all the tumult of a battlefield. Suddenly the bus stopped, and an air-raid warden appeared at the door.

'Everybody off the streets,' he cried. 'They're dropping H.E.'s a mile up the road, and it looks like there's more to come.'

'They're after Howard's Factory, that's what it is,' said a burly woman wisely, leaving the bus with the dignity of a duchess leaving a limousine.

Out on the road, two more air-raid wardens shepherded the passengers to an underground shelter, and the sergeant on forty-eight hours leave irritably rejected the guiding hand of one of them.

'Look here,' he said, 'if it's Howard's Factory they're after, my house is only half a mile from that place. I've just come on leave. I must get home. I must. I must see what's happening.'

He was surprised to hear his own voice: it sounded wild and panic-stricken. He blushed in the darkness and tried to control his feelings. He was trembling.

'That's up to you, soldier,' said the warden calmly.

He was annoyed at being addressed as 'soldier', as if he were an ordinary private, but it was no time to bother about his rank. He broke off at the double, his face and his thoughts set for home. He heard the fall of a bomb a mile ahead, and the buildings on either side of him, the whole street, vibrated dully. Then the ack-ack barrage, silent for a few minutes, began again in a fury of revenge. He kept on running, panting heavily, his heart thumping with the exertion and with alarm. At the corner of Somerdale road he passed a house on fire, where a squad of firemen were fighting incendiaries. He barely looked at them, and changed into a brisk walk: he could run no more. He was out of breath. His walk slackened, and he tried again to control his panic, talking half-aloud to himself in the noisy darkness that was abruptly torn by white and yellow flashes and lit up by the red glow of a fire somewhere far ahead of him.

'Between two fires!' he laughed in the wind hysterically. 'But this is bloody silly of me, this is. Just because a fat dame on the bus says Howard's Factory, I think Lil and the kid are getting it direct. She doesn't know a damn thing about it, any more than I do. Lil's probably safe in the shelter by now, and the kid with her.'

But when he came to the Avenue, the last lap home, he began to run again. Then he stopped, and his heart stopped. His own house was aglow, and he could see half a dozen men racing towards it from the opposite direction, a fire engine behind them. He reached the front door just behind the first of them, a little man with bandy legs.

'Let me in,' he cried excitedly. 'It's my house. I've just come on leave. I've got a wife and kid in there. Let me in!'

'All right, mate, keep cool,' said the fireman. 'Your front door's locked. Have you a key?'

'No, I've no key,' he said impatiently. 'Knock it in, break it open! Do something, don't just stand there!'

They charged the door together, and at the third assault it yielded and they stumbled into the hall, coughing in a thick blue cloud of smoke. He raced to the living-room door, the fireman at his heels.

'Lil!' he shouted frantically. 'Lil! Where are you, Lil? Where's little Elsie, where's the kid?'

He lurched at the door of the living-room, and it would not open. Behind it, he heard the child whimpering in terror and the voice of his wife screaming.

'Davie, get me out! Oh, get me out! The door's jammed—I can't open it—the handle's off!'

'Stand back!' he shouted. 'I'll break it in!'

He stood against the opposite wall of the narrow passage and bracing himself there he put his boot under the handle and exerted all his strength in a short, vicious kick. The door cracked and fell inwards. The perimeter of the room was ablaze, with flames chasing each other up the heavy black-out curtains of the front window, the sewing machine in the corner was burning merrily, and there was a large hole in the ceiling, which seemed ready to fall any minute. In the middle of the floor, his wife stood, pale and trembling, with the child, a toddler of three and a half, in her arms. She rushed to him as he rushed to her, and taking the child from her he got them outside in a hurry. The fireman who had followed him in was already outside, shouting to his team.

'There's nothing we can do in there,' he called, still coughing. 'Get the hose on it from the outside and keep it from spreading—that's the best you can do now.'

He stood at the edge of the pavement with his wife, clear of the firemen. She clung to him moaning, and he hushed her and soothed the child. But they were still badly shaken, and the child wailed beyond comfort.

'I want my daddy's doll! Daddy, I've left my doll!'

Before his wife understood what was going on, he had put the child down and broken away from her, running back to the house. At the gate, the little fireman with the bandy legs stopped him.

'You can't go back in there, mate,' he said plaintively. 'It's all up, I'm sorry. You must have got half a dozen incendiaries in that house. If we can kill it before the whole roof falls in, we'll be bloody lucky.'

'It's all right,' he answered, by-passing the hand that restrained him. 'It won't take me a minute.'

After his panic when he left the bus, he was pleased to find he was quite calm. He felt he simply had to go back into that house to show himself his nerves were under control. The flames were still only along the walls and

curtains, and the doll lay on the carpet unharmed. He ran
in and lifted it quickly, but he did not see that the door
he had kicked in was also on fire now, and as he returned
across the threshold, the crossbeam above the doorway,
burnt by the flames, fell from its place and hit him. It
struck him at the base of the skull, between the ears, and
cracked the cranium. It was the little fireman with the
bandy legs who dragged him out.

When his wife had gone through all the formalities and
informed his unit, she received from his commanding
officer a letter of sympathy, and accompanying the letter
a parcel forwarding all her husband's personal property,
extracted by the quartermaster when he collected the dead
man's kit and equipment. In the house of her mother, the
young widow tenderly examined the contents of the
parcel: the leather writing case she had given him for his
last birthday, a photograph of herself and little Elsie, half
a dozen of her letters, the open razor he had always
preferred to the safety type issued by the army, two of his
pipes and a spare tobacco pouch with some tobacco still
in it, a book she had sent him at Christmas, and a large
envelope containing more letters and photographs. She
took them out slowly, expecting to find they were more
of her own letters, and other photographs of herself, of
their wedding, of the child, old holiday snapshots. But
they were not. She stared at them uncomprehendingly.
They were photographs of an A.T.S. corporal, the same
girl four times over. There was one of her with her cap
on, and she saw an intelligent looking girl with saucy eyes
and a bright smile. There was one of her with her cap off,
and she saw the same smiling girl with a high crown of
hair gleaming with waves. There was one of her
arm-in-arm with her husband, and they looked like two
lovers. There was one of her full-length, alone, and she
saw a tall, handsome girl with a smart appearance and an
attractive figure. Fearfully, she turned them over. On the

back of the first was written in a bold flowing hand: 'To my Favourite Sergeant'. On the back of the second: 'To Davie, with Love from Sheila'. And on the third: 'With all my Heart and all my Love'. On the fourth was written: 'To the Only One I will Ever Love'.

She unfolded the letters, with a feeling of guilt as if her husband could still come in and see her reading what she was never intended to see. They were written by the girl while she was home on leave and addressed to her husband's Camp address. They were all alike, warm, loving and tender, written with the frankness that comes from a love that knows it is returned. She spoke not only of the love she had given but of the love she had received, and in the last of her letters there was a lyrical reference to a week-end she would never forget. The tone of eroticism that marked all the letters was most marked in this one, and ended in a note of ecstasy.

For a full minute the young widow was stunned —speechless, mindless and tearless. Then her lip quivered, and she broke down and sobbed in uncontrollable misery. Her mother came gently to comfort her.

'Put them away, Lil, till another night,' she said. 'You're only hurting yourself. It's too soon to turn over those things.'

'It isn't that, mum,' she wailed. 'It isn't that at all. It's another girl! Look at these—look at these pictures and these letters. He loved me, he didn't love her! I can still hear his voice in my ears when he came looking for me before he broke that door in. He was calling *Lil, Lil, where are you, Lil!*'

She repeated her husband's frantic cry, lingering on the loving labials of her name.

'Oh, mum, he couldn't have loved her! Not from the way he came calling out for me that terrible night. He loved me, mum, it was me he loved. And he loved his little girl too. He gave his life to get Elsie her doll because he knew she loved her daddy's present.'

Her mother was silent, looking in bewildered fascination at the photographs of the A.T.S. corporal and too shy of her daughter's grief to read the love-letters.

Her daughter looked up at her, her weeping stopped for a moment, awed by the mother's silence.

'Maybe he really loved her, and not me at all,' she said slowly.

It's A Wise Child

There were three of us—Prentice, Stratham, and myself. There may have been a fourth, but we never knew who it was, and Kathleen Dalton wouldn't tell. She was only eighteen when it started, and it was all over before she was twenty.

Prentice was the poor boy of the trio. He borrowed money from Stratham as a routine, and for a change he occasionally came to me. His parents had no money, and he was never quite clear as to how he had managed to reach the university or what he was doing there. He was taking commercial science, though I never knew anyone less commercial minded. Stratham was an entirely different proposition. He seemed born for the role of a playboy, until this happened, then he sobered up and settled down. He had plenty of money (anyway, it seemed plenty to Prentice and me), because his father was the boss in a general transport firm, and he was the only son and his mother spoilt him. I myself was doing first-year medical because my father was a doctor. My mother had run away and left him when I was only a kid. I never quite got the story clear, because my father naturally didn't speak much about it, but I gathered that the villain of the piece was a theatrical agent and that my mother just wasn't cut out to be a doctor's wife.

So much for the three of us. We were an ordinary trio of undergraduates, just such a crew as you would meet any year in any university, though of course we thought we were something different, something special. Stratham supplied the finances, Prentice was the comic relief, and I spent my spare time trying to keep them out of trouble.

It isn't so easy to talk about Kathleen Dalton. I discovered her, and innocently mentioned her to Stratham. Prentice was there at the time, and although he didn't seem to be listening he must have heard me all right, for he came along too. After that, I never knew if Stratham or Prentice was the more struck on her, or which she preferred.

It was a morning in May when I first saw her. She worked in a tearoom near the university, a dead little shop that seemed to keep open only because the old woman who owned it lacked the energy to close it. But the magazine crowd, with which Prentice had associations, used it a lot, and it was popular in spasms with the men because it was a handy place to take a girl-friend to between lectures. Kathleen turned up one Monday, and the old woman who had done the serving retired to the kitchen—a move that greatly improved the landscape. She soon became famous, and business picked up at the old place. The first time he saw her, Prentice couldn't stop watching her, and as she moved around her work, he sat in the corner between Stratham and me, and murmured to himself (anything set him off reciting because he knew he had a good voice and like to parade it and show off his memory):

'There's a language in her eye, her cheek, her lip.
Nay, her foot speaks; her wanton spirits look out
Aye every joint and motive of her body.'

She was dark, very dark, with the biggest brown eyes ever you saw, and a lot of dark wavy hair. But it wasn't so much how she looked from the photograph angle; as a matter of fact, her nose was too big for her face if you wanted to be critical. It was how she looked in action, the way she moved, the way she smiled. And she had such a laugh, you could only grin vacuously when you heard it and feel good inside. She was a natural-born actress (which was maybe why Prentice fell for her, he was a bit of an actor and speechifier himself), everything she did was like an exercise in being graceful. She could put more into patting her hair or blowing her nose than most women could put into a love scene under a full moon. She was the only woman ever I saw that could smoke a cigarette properly, and the effortless ease with which she maintained a desultory conversation with a couple of customers as she moved round the tables straightening the chairs, while the summer sun brightened the little tearoom, was a thing of joy.

It was one sleepy afternoon that she told me her lifestory. I had gone there to see her instead of going to the Zoology lab. to cut up a frog. There was nobody else in at that time in the afternoon, and she sat down beside me and smoked a cigarette and talked to me. She acted her story, talking in the beery voice of her father and then answering herself in the shrill nag of her mother. There was nothing much in her story; she was born in a slum, she was the youngest of six, and her father never kept any job long for he wasn't ever sober for long. But talking confidentially like that about herself and her past, she made it clear she had ideals. She was going to get out of the slums, and she was going to get out of them right away, not like her sister. I took it from the way she spoke that her sister wasn't leading a very moral life. Her name was Nora, and she walked out of the happy home when she was nineteen. The others were all boys, and they too had quit. That left our little Kathleen all alone in the old homestead—a room and kitchen in a tenement off the Parliamentary road.

It was this determined respectability of hers that contrasted most to my mind with her debonair bold-eyed manner and dangerous wit. It made Prentice's identification of her nature with that of Cressida's seem a foolish misjudgment. She had a smile and a word for everyone, but her smile was served in different qualities, and there was an ultra-fine discrimination in the way she served it. The first time you saw her, you thought what a fine fellow you must be to get a smile like that from a showpiece like her. But when you saw how she treated the men she knew well, you didn't feel so good about it. Her voice puzzled me. It had no trace of her slum origin; it was low, rich and happy, and she enjoyed using it. She used to get Prentice, who had an inexhaustible stock of quotations, to teach her purple passages which she delighted to declaim like a West End actress. Through sheer devilment, he trained her to recite the words of Ulysses, though I am sure his private application of them never occurred to her. She uttered softly, with appropriate scorn:

'O these encounterers, so glib of tongue,
That give a costing welcome ere it comes,
And wide unclasp the tables of their thoughts
To every ticklish reader! Set them down
For sluttish spoils of opportunity
And daughters of the game.'

'A woman of quick sense,' he murmured when she picked it up easily and I felt there was an unnecessary wealth of bitterness in his veiled quotation of Nestor's comment on Cressida.

But those were happy days compared with what followed. In the autumn, when we returned after the long vacation, Kathleen returned too; and before winter came, those days of easy friendliness and idle chatter seemed to belong to a pleasant dream from which we had long ago awakened. I knew that Prentice was taking her out, though I don't know where he got the money from apart from what he could borrow from Stratham. He no longer spoke of her as a Cressida, though since Kathleen herself never appreciated the drive of those allusions, I don't suppose she noticed any change. Yet all the time, I felt it was only a morbid fascination that could not last, and I never believed he had any real affection or any real respect for her.

It was bad enough when she got herself involved with Prentice, taking up valuable time with a student who wasn't her style at all (though Prentice liked to use the line that they were both children of the people—this peculiarly foolish remark being an allusion to his own poverty-stricken background, of which he was unduly conscious), but when she got involved with Stratham too, I sat back and sighed and waited for trouble.

I never discussed her with Stratham and Prentice after I first told them about her, and they had no idea how I felt, but whatever impression she had made on them was trivial compared with what she had done to me. Since they had got there first, and since I disliked competition and usually kept my thoughts to myself, I watched developments silently, suffering helplessly like a dumb animal. In any case, my mother's history had made me very chary of women.

Maybe I got more out of it that way than the other way, for she confided in me right to the end, more than in the other two. I don't know how she managed to string them both along for so many months, keeping each in ignorance of the other's share. I don't know how they missed it, though Prentice was so conceited that his vanity often blinded him to the obvious, and for all his good points Stratham was a simple-minded fellow who took things at their face value. It flattered me too that she made no secret of it to me, taking it for granted that although I was their friend I would not pass on to them the knowledge she had given me in confidence. I knew she confided in me more than she did in them, because when they spoke about her in my presence I saw every time that I knew far more about her background, her upbringing, her joys and sorrows, her dreams and ambitions, than they did. So I felt closer to her. I was on her side all the time, and I couldn't blame her no matter what she did.

I tried to quiz her once as to how it squared with the ideals she had confessed to me, how it fitted in with her ambition to get out of the slums and live a sedate life in one of the city's suburbs, married to a sober young man with prospects. It was obvious to me that neither Stratham nor Prentice would ever marry her; and even if either of them ever got the idea, it would take years before it became possible. But it wasn't easy to talk to her about that, or to say she was only wasting her time and running the risk of spoiling her future. I could hardly tell her that to carry out her own plans, she ought to be looking out for the industrious young man of her dreams instead of wasting her time on a couple of students who wouldn't earn a penny for years. When I tried to put the situation tactfully to her one afternoon and force her to think clearly, she picked me up on it right away and said, laughing at me:

'But good heavens, boy, it's not a question of wasting my time. I'm not going to propose to either of them. And if either of them proposed to me, I'd be stricken dumb with amazement.'

After that, I couldn't ask her what she expected to get out of it all. Apparently, she didn't expect anything, except maybe experience—which I suspected she did not lack. So I gave it up.

It was spring again before Stratham and Prentice discovered they had only a share in Kathleen Dalton, not a monopoly of her. Prentice found it out first, and he was furious. I didn't mind so much his attempt to pick a quarrel with Stratham as the way he spoke of Kathleen. It was simply absurd in its bitterness and stupid in its contemptuous ranting. It surprised me, for I had thought he was too literate, too self-conscious in his restraint, to go in for the silly complaints of a jilted adolescent. But there was no talking to him.

'You don't know the half of it,' he retorted abruptly. 'You don't know what there was between us. The best thing you can do is keep out of this.'

Stratham, on the other hand, seemed too amazed to speak, and I don't think he ever appreciated the irony of the situation, that it was mainly on the money he had lent him that Prentice had ever been able to take Kathleen out at all. He took a lot of aggressive chatter from Prentice, but kept himself under control and simply ignored the efforts Prentice made to start a fight. There was considerable coolness between them for several weeks, but in the end Stratham's attitude broke down our friend's insolence and they were as familiar as ever with each other.

Meanwhile, poor Kathleen wandered round the tables as if she were walking in her sleep. I could see her mind was not on her work, and her smile to her customers became an artificial thing, as tedious as an advertisement, without vitality or significance. Prentice and Stratham no longer came in, and since she didn't ask me why or wherefore, I took it she knew quite well what had happened. She spoke to me one morning when the place was quiet and I sat in the corner praying she would come over and speak to me. She came along after judicious delay and made no attempt to take my order.

'Aren't they ever going to come in again?' she asked in a low, miserable voice.

'I'm sure I don't know,' I said.

'Oh, they're a pair of damn fools,' she muttered. 'What do you want?'

And that was all. It was in May, exactly a year after I had first set eyes on her, that I suddenly realised there was something wrong. I can still remember the way my heart jumped as I looked at her and knew what the matter was and wondered why I hadn't noticed it before. I didn't have to be a medical student to diagnose her condition; it was plain to everybody. The girl was pregnant. I tried to speak to her, but she had no talk for me at all. She served me and got rid of me as quickly as she could. It was no longer the bold-eyed Kathleen Dalton of a year ago, no longer the merry actress whose eyes reflected an infinite happiness, whose smile expressed an overflow of joy, of fond affection for all mankind. Even her beautiful hair seemed neglected. Her whole expression was as vacuous as a mirror with nobody in front of it, her airs and graces all gone, her very movement betraying a defeated spirit.

By the end of May, the rumours of her condition were all over the university, the subject of coarse jokes to the lightminded and of hushed whispers of horror to the moralists. Prentice came to me in a state of panic one morning as I was leaving the Anatomy lab. where I had been dissecting a dead man's hand. He almost beseeched me to say the rumours were all nonsense.

'No,' I said, 'it was obvious a month ago. But I didn't think it was necessary for me to inform you.'

He looked at me straight for a long while before he replied, and then he spoke in a slow and serious voice.

'Look here,' he said. 'I never see her now. I don't know what's going on. You ought to have told me. As for this—this business, I'm as innocent as the unborn babe itself. All I want to know is, where can I find Stratham?'

Before he saw Stratham, Stratham had seen me. Our dialogue merely repeated what I had had with Prentice, and Stratham left me to go in search of the man who was searching for him, looking like the hero in a Victorian melodrama going out into the night to hunt down the villain.

It left me not knowing what to think. That Stratham and Prentice were equally innocent seemed certain from their whole manner, from the very way they reacted to the news, but I don't know if either of them believed the other. I know they both appealed to Kathleen—but she wouldn't tell. They never spoke to each other again, and all my efforts to reconcile them were completely unsuccessful. Then, before the month of June was out, Kathleen left without a word of warning to me beforehand, and I never saw her again.

I can look back on it now, after these last seventeen years and not feel a thing about it. But at the time, I admit, it was a damnable shock to me, and I took a long time to get over it. Maybe I've never managed to get over it, or maybe my mother's history is to blame. But anyway, I have never married and am not likely to marry now. The women that set out to be pleasant to me only bored me. I never again saw a woman that was anywhere near Kathleen Dalton for looks and wit and sheer personality. Those that had the looks had neither the wit nor the personality; and those that had the wit and personality hadn't her looks. I could no more be impressed by them, when I remembered Kathleen Dalton, than you could be impressed by the lyrics of Irving Berlin after you had been reading Shakespeare's sonnets. I know it made a tremendous difference to Stratham, and for a long time the young women of his west-end set thought him really queer, he was so sublimely uninterested in all their wiles and smiles. He was over thirty before the quiet daughter of a Glasgow shipowner, a ruthless wench who had always got her own way, finally broke down his defences and persuaded him to meet her at the altar four years ago. Prentice hadn't married when I last saw him; I know that after he graduated he worked with the I.C.I. for a little while, and then he quit and went into journalism. In 1937 he was in Spain, covering the war from the Republican side. Today, I think, he is a war correspondent somewhere in China.

But it is time I finished this. I wouldn't have started it at all, if it hadn't been for what happened last night. Six or seven months after the war started, I turned over my practice to my father and joined the army. After knocking about various stations in the Middle East, I was posted as medical officer to a camp in the Midlands. It was there I met Steinberg again. He was an American Jew who had taken his medical degree with me away back in the late nineteen-twenties—lots of those American Jews came over to our Scottish universities in those days, and then returned to the States when they had graduated. I had worked with Steinberg in the old days, and I was very glad to catch up on him again. We had a lot to talk about too; he was medical officer in a camp of American soldiers a few miles from our troops, and he had put in six months service in North Africa.

I was going back to his Mess with him last night for a quiet drink, and as we approached the camp I saw a girl, a mere slip of a thing about seventeen or eighteen, loitering at the gate. I stopped in my tracks and my stomach turned over. It was Kathleen Dalton to the life.

'What's the matter?' said Steinberg.

'Nothing,' I said. 'But I think I need that drink you promised me.'

As we passed through the gate, the loitering girl looked

us up and down, and flashed a smile on us. If the idea hadn't been so absurd (after all, I was old enough to be her father), I would have sworn she was preparing to accost us. Just inside the gate, a sergeant of the regimental police was standing alongside the guard, and when he saluted Steinberg, my colleague said to him breezily:

'How's the pain in your shoulder, sergeant?'

'Oh, I've got rid of that, sir,' said the sergeant. 'It's a pain in the neck I've got now—that kid at the gate. She's been here every night this week, stopping our men. We just can't get rid of her.'

'Can't you book her?' said Steinberg.

'No, she never crosses the line,' said the sergeant. 'The civil police got her a while ago under the Vagrancy Act, and she got a month in clink. But she's back again. She knows all the answers. She won't leave our boys alone.'

'What is it our American soldiers have that attracts your girls?' asked Steinberg frivolously.

'I wouldn't know,' I said, 'unless it's the Almighty Dollar. But I want to talk to that girl.'

I left him and went through the gate again. The girl retreated a step as I came out, and then the wary look left her face and she turned on her smile again.

'What's your name, missie?' I said, and even before she spoke I knew the answer. That smile proclaimed it.

'Kathleen Dalton,' she said, and the very voice was Kathleen Dalton's. 'Though I don't see what business it is of yours.'

'How did you get from Glasgow to this place?' I asked.

The wary look returned to her eyes. Her smile was cut off, suddenly, as you turn off a light.

'How do you know I come from Glasgow?' she said slowly, bewildered.

'Maybe it was your Cockney accent,' I said, watching her closely.

'Don't you be funny about my voice,' she said quietly.

'My mother taught me how to speak so as no one would know where I came from.'

'Tell me,' I said, 'is your mother still living?'

'Why do you want to know?' she demanded, retreating another step. 'You seem to know too much already.'

'I used to know your mother,' I said.

'Oh, I see, that's it!' she intoned wisely. 'Maybe you're my father?'

'Don't you know who your father was?' I replied. 'Didn't your mother ever tell you?'

'Listen, mister,' she said, 'I don't know who you are, but you ask too many questions. You're not a policeman, are you?'

I shook my head.

'I'm only a poor doctor,' I said. 'But I was once your mother's friend, seventeen years ago, when I was a medical student in Glasgow.'

'Then you should know who my father was,' retorted the girl quickly, eyeing me thoughtfully. 'All she ever told me was, he was a student and his father was well off, and she thought he would marry her and make a fine lady of her.'

She stopped and looked at the ground, tracing an arc in the gravel with the toe of her right foot.

'Well, it didn't come off,' she said in a low voice.

I could see it would take little to make her hysterical, and although she was prettily dressed her clothes were old, and she was obviously a bad case of malnutrition.

'I don't know what happened,' she muttered rapidly. 'All I know is, my mother took a gamble, and it didn't come off. But I'm going to get out of this, I'm getting out of this country. I'm going to get my own life in my own house. I'm going to marry an American soldier and go to America with him when the war's over. I can wait. But I'm not going to be poor all my days. I'm going to get out of this, and you can't stop me—even if you are my father.'

An Angel In His House

She was very much in love with him, but whether her excess
of love made her doubt if so much could be returned, or
whether she had in fact the intuition ascribed to her sex, she
had no faith in his feelings for her. She was only twenty, and
her reading was limited to women's weeklies. When she
indulged in serious conversation, it went to her head and
she staggered round the twin topics of the nature of man
and the existence of true love. Like other metaphysicians,
she never came to any conclusion about either.

He was one of her schoolgirl idols when she was in the
fourth form and he was in the sixth, and it was a great
pleasure to her that, when they had both risen to the rank
of former pupils, he paid her so much attention at a
reunion dance. They went about together for a year after
that, and her troubles with him confirmed her tendency
to look at life in terms of potted wisdom, as 'You've got
to take the rough with the smooth'; 'There's no such thing
as real love', and 'Men are brutes'. He had set out on a
university course as a medical student, but the change in
domestic circumstances after the death of his father
forced him to find a job at once and he went to work near
the university in a shop that sold medical text-books. He
was tall, fair, in boisterous good health, fond of practical
jokes, rather coarse, and altogether a knowledgeable
young man.

So knowledgeable he alarmed her, and his brashness led her to put an end to their friendship. At least she tried to, but all she meant was that he should put an end to his extreme demands on her and continue more sedately. He chose to see no alternative, and while she sat at home waiting for him to call, thinking he understood and accepted what she meant, he found a nurse in the Western Infirmary to please him. When it became clear that he was not coming back, she wept in bed every night for a month and then wilted a little, getting her compensation for the episode by looking upon herself as a woman wise beyond her years, old before her time, experienced beyond her mother's suspicions.

Before another year was out, she heard from her friends that he was always asking about her, and one of them obligingly gave him the telephone number of her new office. She was not unprepared for his voice when he telephoned her late one autumn afternoon, and yet she had difficulty with her breath and feared he could hear her heart. The conversation was slightly stilted. They were embarrassed, falling into gaps in the uneven terrain of their manœuvring, then scrambling out with a self-conscious hum and a haw. After five minutes beating about the bush, he put the question to her and she agreed to see him again.

Soon it was as bad as ever, but although she said she had learned her lesson and told him he would never again break her heart by walking out on her because she would keep her heart to herself, all she had in fact learned was she could not do without him. She had just been getting used to it when he telephoned, and not only the depressing dullness of that state, but the long journey she had made to get there, seemed to her equally unthinkable again.

Of course she was often happy with him, simply and untroubledly happy, and there were evenings when he was content to hold her hand in the pictures and no more, and she thought that was wonderful, but it never lasted.

'You know,' she told her confidant in the audit office, Mr. Barlow, 'I'd be perfectly happy just to listen to him talking, just to sit beside him at the fire. But him! He's different.'

It became so bad again that she thought she would have to leave him for good, for her own good. But she was determined that this time he would not leave her under the pretext of failing to see the alternative she offered; she would do the leaving, without any alternative, and frankly and firmly tell him she could not and would not go on. She burst out with it impulsively one evening when he hedged about coming round to her parents two nights later, on New Year's Eve. He knew them already, he had no reason to be shy—her father in particular liked him, but still he hedged. He spoke as if the Scotch custom of a family gathering at Hogmanay was silly, too ridiculous for him to follow.

'You'd think we weren't good enough for you, the way you talk,' she said angrily. 'You're selfish, utterly selfish. You want everything your way, but will you do the least thing for me? No, never! I don't believe you could ever love anybody but yourself. It's the one thing all the time with you. all you do is rush at things, and you never think of anybody else's feelings. The best thing we can do is to stop seeing each other.'

To her dismay he agreed at once. He said, not without a touch of gallantry, that she was too much for him. She would have preferred him to say too good, but he said too much. He could not resist her. It was dangerous to be alone with her, and lately they had managed too many evenings alone. She was quite right; it would be better if they stopped seeing each other.

'Otherwise it can only end in disaster,' he ended remotely.

Only her astonishment kept her from weeping on the

spot. She was almost hysterical at the calmness with which he announced he could not be calm in her company, at the complacency with which he took her impulsive suggestion that they should stop meeting. His attitude illuminated for her the insincerity of her proposal, and that, too, was an additional pain. She had thought she was sincere when she mediated it, and she could not understand how it became any the less sincere simply because it found an unguarded expression. She almost shook him as she stood clutching his lapels in their good-night embrace, standing at the porch with him at midnight, the two of them behind the half-closed storm-doors and she with her back to the hall-door.

'It's all very well for you,' she said. 'It's just what I said. You don't care for anybody but yourself. You'd like to pick me up and drop me just whenever it suits you. You could go away tonight and not bother your head if you never saw me again.'

'It was your idea in the first place,' he said stolidly.

In the end they agreed to meet again on New Year's Eve to discuss the proposal that they should not meet again. By habit they made to go to a cinema, but there were queues everywhere, and because it was cold and wet, he said they should go to his mother's house. She had been there before, mildly welcomed by a widow who seemed distracted from matters immediately in front of her and continually casting some unuttered calculation. So she agreed meekly enough; perhaps they would come by half an hour alone while his mother pottered and panned in the kitchen, and they could settle their future in a heart-to-heart talk, or perhaps he would not want to settle it and everything would go on as before. She dimly saw that she didn't know what she wanted, and as they trudged to his mother's house, there was a narrow chasm of silence between them, so easy to cross if she just looked at it rationally, but impossible for her to leap first, and he said nothing.

Then, to her embarrassment, the widow gave her a welcome even more remote than usual; her unfinished calculation seemed more retrospective than ever, and to make her position worse, she was quickly aware that the mother and son were on bad terms. As she waited alone in the front room at a pleasant enough fire, she could hear them in the kitchen carrying on from where they had left off. The mother came through to get a scarf, and without open rudeness ignored her and went back to the kitchen. she heard the son's brusque voice and the mother's sharp reply.

'When you come back from Hilda's,' he was saying.

'If I come back,' snapped the mother.

She heard the front door bang and felt prickly with discomfort.

He came through to her calmly.

'What's wrong?' she asked timidly.

'Oh, nothing,' he said, and kissed her warmly. 'Just one of her moods.'

There was no discussion, no heart-to-heart talk to settle their future. She was always weak when he attacked her, and her muddle about what she wanted made her weaker. He started at once making love to her in the same old way, and she tried for a moment to keep him off with a cold, astonished question.

'How can you? You quarrel with your mother like that, you let her go without even trying to make it up—oh, you're selfish! You think of nobody but yourself. And on New Year's Eve too!'

He slowed down and became all gentle and explanatory. It was a silly little quarrel. It meant nothing. She was often like that. She said things she didn't mean. She would come back as if nothing had happened. She always went round to see Hilda, his married sister, when she was cross with him, and stayed there till bedtime.

'How could I leave you?' he asked fondly. 'You don't want me to leave you, now do you? Tell me the truth.'

The reconciliation he offered was too much for her. He had crossed the narrow chasm of silence, and they stood on the same side, murmuring loving words together, mutually caressing. Within half an hour he had overcome her scruples and had his way. She held out as long as she could, exercising an effort she felt in herself was terrific, but in one last moment, as he persisted, she loosened her grasp and she was beaten and no longer cared.

After it was all over, she wept for ten minutes, and privately wondered what she was fussing about. She was disappointed in herself, that she had done what she had sworn she would never do, and disappointed in what she had done, that it was hardly worth so much curiosity, so much fighting, so much excitement. But he came back to her gratefully, and she took the chance to coax him to come round to her parents after all. He still jibbed at the idea, and she had to break away from him forcibly and threaten to go home alone, to go and get her hat and coat and show she was serious, before he finally agreed to accompany her. The party was warmed up when they arrived, crowded and noisy, for her father was a sociable man. She sat in a corner and drank more than was good for her, and when her seducer stood up to leave the party he had never wanted to attend, she startled the company by mouthing drunkenly, 'Don't let him go! Don't let him go! If he goes away, I'll never see him again.'

She began to cry, talking away to herself indistinctly, and everybody asked everybody else who had given her all the drink. But since it was Hogmanay and nobody was quite sober, her condition was looked upon as amusing rather than serious, the more so since young love was always a topic for a joke.

She was back at work on the second day of the New Year and felt an urge to confide in Mr. Barlow again. She had to wait till after lunch to get him alone, and slipped away from the canteen back to her seat in the typing pool with her knitting. Mr. Barlow sat in the farthest corner. He never went to the canteen, but lunched at his supervisor's table from a flask that contained something that wasn't tea and a package of rye bread. There was supposed to be something wrong with his stomach. He was middle-aged, or looked it, and if he was married, widowed, divorced or single, nobody knew. He listened but said little. Perhaps that was why she had got into the habit of returning early from her lunch to chat with him alone. She could never have said if she even as much as liked him; he was beyond liking or disliking. But he had always kept her secrets, and the little he said made her feel friendly. He was like a wall that looks adequate, not a splendid piece of architecture, but the right height to lean on.

She parked her knitting and her bag, took off her coat and strolled up to him.

'Hello, Helen,' he said, putting his flask away and screwing up the paper bag that had carried his sandwiches. No one ever actually saw him eat, but it was assumed he did so since he was apparently still alive.

She sat down across the table from him and plunged into the heart of it.

'It's all over, finished, *zu Ende*,' she said. Having once found he understood her fifth-form German, she occasionally used to him such phrases as she could remember.

He looked at her deeply and waited.

She told him all she could as openly as she could, getting round the difficulty of directly telling him she had lost her chastity by saying, 'So when his mother went out we were all alone till near on midnight, and you can think what you like.'

Whatever he thought, he said nothing. She blurted on.

'Well, anyway, I know what I'm missing now. And it's not worth all that much.'

'I agree,' he said. 'But it's a pity you had to find it out that way.'

She took a cigarette from him sadly and he looked at her curiously as he lit it. She had good looks but no beauty, a strong body and a wilful mouth.

'But why are you so sure it's all over?' he asked. 'All that talk of ending it was before you—'

He stopped and left it without words.

'I know,' she said. 'But—oh, I don't know. I don't know what's in his mind.'

Because they seemed to encourage her a little, he repeated some commonplace words of comfort he did not believe, and out of simple kind-heartedness, he elaborated his platitudes, looking at her eyes and marvelling at the burden women took upon themselves in the name of love. She sat staring into the future, and he saw she was at once frightened and allured by the threat of motherhood. The worry in her eyes faded as he chattered on, speaking to her at length for once, and he was amazed to see it go so quickly. He was certain that even if her conqueror did telephone her during the week, he would not take long after that to arrange his exit; or if he ever did marry her, which he could not believe, then indeed

> No sweet aspersions would the heavens let fall
> To make that contract grow, but barren hate,
> Sour-eyed disdain and discord would bestrew
> The union of their bed with weeds so loathly
> That they would hate it both...

But instead of saying so, he said gently, making the sentimentality palatable with an ironic smile. 'No, don't you worry. You'll be all right. I'll live to see you engaged at the summer and married at Christmas. And you'll be a loving, attentive wife, an angel in the house, and you'll send him out with his trousers pressed, and you'll polish his shoes for him and—'

'Oh no,' she interrupted him quickly. 'Oh no! That's one thing I'll never do. I can't imagine anything more servile. There are some things I wouldn't do for any man, and polishing his shoes is one of them.'

A Friend Of Humanity

He was determined to improve his position in life, an aim his father daily recommended to him in those words, and also (again in the words of his father) to be of service to humanity. He stayed at school to matriculation level, and after some blind-alley clerking, he went into the army. He came out with his ideals unchanged and his vocabulary increased, and on his father's suggestion he applied for admission to a training college for teachers.

'A good lad like you is just what's wanted,' said his father. 'A lad with your education and your tastes in life could do a lot of good for boys.'

Mr. Glanders had a small newsagent's shop, inherited from a maiden aunt. He had broadened his mind by reading all the periodicals he sold and his son seemed to him like a sixpenny weekly, well-informed on foreign affairs, up-to-date in modern literature, knowledgeable on films and the theatre, and well worth any ratepayer's money.

'After all, what's the use of learning things if you don't pass them on?' he asked. 'Sharing knowledge, that's what's got mankind where they are today. You should write to the education offices and tell them all about yourself.'

So young Mr. Glanders wrote a letter and was called for an interview by the director of studies. He went for a haircut, pressed his trousers, took his military carriage, and arrived in good time to find fourteen men already waiting. When he entered the director's room half an hour later, he stood to attention till he was asked to sit down. In a weary voice the director explained that, although there was a shortage of teachers, places for students were not numerous, and it was his duty to make sure that only suitable candidates were allowed to begin training. Perhaps Mr. Glanders would like to tell him why he wanted to be a teacher. The request was made more to hear how Mr. Glanders spoke than to hear what he had to say, but the young man missed that. He began away back in his boyhood, and while the director noted the breadth and pitch of the vowels, the vigour of the consonants and the rate and diction, the candidate went earnestly on.

The accent was passable, the director decided, and although the speaker would never entirely lose his more subtle variances from standard English, the class in phonetics would make him sufficiently alert to avoid obvious errors when he was speaking for show. But he couldn't stop the gush of words, and being temperamentally polite, he went on doodling patiently until annoyance at being lectured by a novice on the history and theory of education made him say with sudden vigour, 'Yes, that will do, Mr. Glanders. I'll let you know.'

'John Locke says in his Essay on Education,' said Mr. Glanders, 'that it doesn't matter what a man says or thinks if he says or thinks only what he is directed by another.' But I think there's a fallacy there. Because if you take a person who knows something better than another person, surely it's his duty to direct him. You take the case of a teacher. Now how is education possible if——'

He had never read Locke on Education, but he had seen the tag ascribed to Locke in a Reader's Digest and the

Essay on Education seemed the likeliest place for it. It was a clever move, he thought, to let the director see he knew about Locke and had opinions of his own too. The director said 'Yes' again, stood up, held out his hand, and took him quickly to the door.

In spite of his garrulity, he was admitted to the training college, and became prominent in weekly debates and classroom discussions, gaining a session's notoriety for his disputatious dogmatism and his constant appeal to the general good of mankind as his arbiter. To anyone who opposed his ideas he bluntly retorted, 'You don't know what you're talking about, old boy. You just don't understand the matter.' He was (he told the lecturer in political philosophy) wholeheartedly in favour of liberty and the free state, but it was the place of the teacher to educate the child to liberty, and a state could not be free if its children were not properly educated, that is, trained to act in accordance with the general good of mankind. He signed a peace manifesto and spoke at a students' debate in favour of disarmament, arguing that education meant peace and peace meant education, and since he was interested in education, he was interested in peace.

When he passed his last examination and emerged proudly as a certificated non-graduate teacher, he went to work in a council school with a class of boys aged thirteen. His antics on the first morning amused them, but he interpreted their hilarity as a natural response to his fresh style, and their familiarity he regarded as the simple expression of the love that answers love.

'You've got to love boys if you're going to work with them,' he said that evening to his girl-friend. 'I've struck up an understanding with them right away. They know me and I know them. Before I've done with them, they'll have a good grasp of the nature of the modern world.

They'll be able to take their place in it and carry on the fight for peace and freedom and the general good of mankind.'

'Yes,' she answered as they stood down the lane and waited for the dark.

Next day he carried on from where he had left off, playing the genial father, though sometimes during the morning he wondered if the geniality were not just a little too mutual. In the last lap of the afternoon he came to his history lesson. He was supposed to be doing the Tudors, but he didn't see what they had to do with the modern world, so he hurried past them to the Civil War and then by a mighty leap crossed the Channel to the French Revolution, solemnly explaining the necessity for the reign of terror. Proud of his eloquence, he returned to Britain to speak of the Reform Bills and the rise of the toiling masses in whose hands lay the future of mankind. In a magnificent peroration he emphasised the duty of all right-thinking people to support the forces making for peace in a world where human beings were still ruthlessly exploited by the greed of men who would commit any atrocity to further their own selfish ends.

He finished his lecture oblivious of the remote inattention he had gained, his voice tired, but his conscience glowing warm inside him at a good job well done. He had contributed his mite towards the improvement of humanity. If everyone did what he did, he was sure the next generation of citizens would avoid the blunders of their fathers.

There were still ten minutes left and it occurred to him that if the class wrote down a few dates, it would help to kill the time, though he considered facts were less important than the broad sweep of events. He went to the blackboard, explaining his purpose over his shoulder, and listed his favourite topics: the English Civil War, the French Revolution, the Industrial Revolution, the Reform Bills. Speaking the words as he wrote, he was beginning to write next, the Russian Revolution, when somebody shouted in a bogus voice, 'Oh, sir, your shirt's hanging out!'

He had for some time been worried at the glossiness of the seat of his trousers (the first thing he meant to buy out of his first pay was a new suit), and in a panic reaction his hand darted to his backside. He found the cloth still whole and the way he had revealed his alarm infuriated him even more than the insolence of the interruption.

He turned round, nearer white than red, but nobody in front of him seemed to have heard anything. Some who were writing looked up at the blackboard to see what to copy next; others who were looking at the blackboard looked down again at their books to write what they had just taken in. On every face was innocence, every boy a simian trinity incarnate. He knew it was no use asking who had said his shirt was hanging out. He looked and looked at them but none of them looked at him. Their silence loudly asserted they had seen nothing, heard nothing, said nothing. He turned again to his blackboard, trembling a little.

When the class had finished writing, he went over the dates again and then in a mannerism he had picked up from army instructors he asked stiffly, 'Any questions?'

Floyd's hand went up.

'Yes?' said Mr. Glanders, his rage receding as he prepared to descend and be of service to humanity.

'Please sir, is Glanders your right name?'

'Why do you ask that? What's that got to do with what I'm trying to teach you?' he said impatiently.

'The professor says it's a disease,' said Floyd.

'The professor?' he asked, suspicious and stern. He felt something flow from him, a magic and a power he could not regain, perhaps had never had, felt as it may be an Ashanti chieftain feels when for some failure his tribe pull him off the royal stool and de-sanctify him by making him touch the common earth with his holy rump.

Floyd pointed to Hooper, small, sharpnosed and spectacled, a bookish boy.

'It says here,' Hooper said without rising, 'glanders, a malignant——'

'Says where?' Mr. Glanders shouted, tormented. 'What's that you've got there?'

'A dictionary,' Hooper answered grudgingly, in the manner of one stupidly asked to explain the obvious.

'And what are you doing with a dictionary when we're supposed to be doing history?' Mr. Glanders screamed.

'Please sir, you gave them out,' Hooper said soothingly. 'Remember? So as we could find out the meaning of enfranchisement for ourselves. It says, glanders: a malignant, contagious and fatal disease of horses.'

'Put that book away and be sensible,' Mr. Glanders ordered fiercely. 'The lowest form of wit is to make fun of somebody else's name. Would you think it funny if I said a hooper was a wild swan? Hooper is a name for a kind of swan. Did you know that?'

'No sir. I think that's very interesting,' Hooper replied gratefully. 'Is that because it goes *whoop*?'

He gave an abrupt loud whoop that made everybody jump, and waited for an answer.

Mr. Glanders walked blindly across to his desk, put away his history book, and in a frenzied effort at self-control turned to face his class. Spasmodic whoops were coming from all round the room.

'Maybe you think you're clever. Maybe you think you're funny,' he began, his voice erratic, addressing Hooper alone in the hope that the others would be quiet if he ignored them. 'You think it's interesting that a hooper is a swan, do you? I'll tell you what to think. And

I'll tell you when to think it too. I'll have some respect here!'

His anger howled inside him and came out like a tornado. He realised he was shouting louder than he had ever shouted in his life before, and with a passing perplexity he felt that shouting louder was making him angrier. Yet he had to shout louder to make his voice rise over the whoops and shrieks of sheer merriment that were the revenge for boredom, the reward for his attempt to direct them what to think. The thought suddenly arose, making it all clear and absolving him from blame, that these were not boys of the right kind at all; they were boys who didn't deserve his genial rule of reason. First they must become enlightened and then they would deserve the freedom he had planned for them. But how they were ever to become enlightened if they weren't attracted by his instruction, he couldn't clearly see. All he knew was that, from now on, they were at war, and, turning from Hooper for a minute, he directed the heavy artillery of his insults and threats against the rest of his class.

But the abuse he bawled at them was too small a vent for his temper. He had to do something, to bring them to their knees and keep them there, and driven by a necessity that trampled unseeingly over all discretion, he strode over to Hooper and boxed his ears.

'You think you're a swan, do you?' he roared. 'You're not a swan, you're a rat! An ill-bred, insolent, little rat!'

At every stress in his closing crescendo he struck again and Hooper cowered back, trying to get his hand between his ear and the repeated blows. The reign of terror had started.

Angela's Brother

Terry had protected Angela since the morning he took her by the hand across the busy road to start her first day at school. She was five then, and he was seven. He took the place of a father who was dead and forgotten and gave Angela his daily devotion. He was proud of his little sister.

She was a dark-haired brown-eyed child, slender and pretty. When she was growing up he tried to rule her and guide her. Nobody else bothered.

Their mother was a careless woman. At week-ends she was never quite sober. She came home from the pub on a Saturday night with a carry-out and a couple of cronies, singing the songs of the Glasgow-Irish till past midnight.

Terry had no use for her when she was in that state. He gave her respect because she was his mother, but that was all. He was an earnest lad who wanted to get out of the violence and bigotry of his native district. He wanted Angela to be well-spoken and good-mannered, like himself. His secret dream was that with her good looks, and if she would only get the habit of good speech and get a good job, she would one day meet a good man and make a good marriage, and so she would escape from Tordoch.

He scolded her when she was rude to her mother. He told her bad manners weren't nice in a pretty girl. And when she started coming in late at night after she left school he always asked her where she had been and who was with her.

He looked on himself as head of the house, and put aside as something best forgotten his failure to have any influence on his young brother Danny. His mother blamed him for giving all his attention to Angela, though Danny was younger than Angela and also needed watching. He defended himself by saying a girl needs more protection than a boy, and Danny should have been able to take care of himself.

Now Danny was serving two years in a detention centre for assault, after a year's probation for OLP and HB. He was sixteen when he was put away. Angela was seventeen, and that was when her trouble started.

She was never exactly insolent to Terry, but she jibbed at his attempt to keep her on a tight rein. She told him lies about where she had been and the company she was keeping. He was easily deceived. He might have known or guessed more if he hadn't been staying at home every night reading books from the library to improve his general knowledge. He had done well at school and passed a test to get a job in National Security. His ambition was to take another test that would get him upgraded, and then he might be able to take his mother and Angela to a better district.

It was Angela's moodiness at the turn of the year that upset him. His eyes were never off her when she moved about the house. He wanted her to stop sulking. If he spoke first she hardly answered. It hurt him.

He was afraid he had lost for ever the slim little trusting sister he used to take by the hand at a dangerous crossing. Anxiously watching her, he began to think her breasts were bigger and her hips were broader than seemed to suit her. He didn't like to think what he was thinking, but he couldn't leave it unsaid. It was his duty to know, and help her. He brooded for a week, then spoke to her timidly when they were alone in the house one rainy Saturday night the week before Christmas.

'Are you all right, Angela?'

'Why shouldn't I be?' she snapped.

'That's not what I'm asking,' he said, gentle and patient.

'Then what are you asking? Or trying to ask. But you're too frightened to say it.'

'Say what?'

He was alarmed. She seemed to know what he was thinking.

'You think I'm pregnant, don't you? Well, so I am.'

He asked her who it was, but she wouldn't say. For the first time in his life he lost his temper with her. He shook her and thumped her. He twisted her arm till she screamed.

'I want his name,' he shouted.

'Mick Nolan,' she sobbed.

'That hooligan!'

He shoved her away. He was trembling.

Angela wiped her eyes with the back of her hand.

'He's not a hooligan. He's a good boy. I love him. And he loves me. He told me.'

'Then he'll marry you?' said Terry.

'No,' said Angela, dry-eyed and calm.

'By God he will,' said Terry.

'No he won't,' said Angela, and went to her bed.

Terry sat up till his mother came home from the pub. Drunk or sober, she had to be told. Arrangements had to be made. Marriage to a local hood wasn't the kind of marriage he had dreamt of for Angela, but he thought it was the only way to diminish her disgrace.

His mother was curt when he told her.

'Aye, I know. She's three months gone. So what?'

'So what are we going to do about it?'

'What do you expect me to do? I'll have to look after

it when it's born, and let Angela get back to work.'

She poured a can of export into a tumbler and lamented.

'I'll be Granny Rooney, and me no forty yet.'

'She says it's Mick Nolan,' said Terry.

'Who else would it be?' It's him she was going with. At least he's a Catholic.'

Terry stared at her, breathing deep in anger.

'What difference does that make?'

'It means the baby'll no have any Protestant blood,' his mother swayed as she answered.

'Look, mother,' said Terry, patient again. 'There's A blood and there's B blood and there's O blood. But there's no such thing as Protestant blood.'

'That's what you think,' she replied with the scorn of drunk wisdom. 'When you're my age you'll know better.'

'She says he won't marry her,' said Terry.

His mother shrugged, tired of the conversation.

'Why the hell should he? It's her to blame.'

'But she'll have to get married.'

'Why? You make too much of that girl. You always did.'

'I want to see her married,' said Terry. 'I want to see a husband's name on the birth certificate.'

His mother laughed. She raised her glass to him, mocking.

'That's right, son! Defend the family honour!'

Then she turned on him bitterly.

'Though who cares nowadays? Least of all in Tordoch. Sure, everybody says it's the worst scheme in Glasgow. The lowest of the low finish up here.'

'You don't have to tell me that,' said Terry. 'I wanted to see Angela get out of it one day.'

'Then it will be the best thing for the pair of them if Mick Nolan won't marry her.'

'But he will,' said Terry. 'I'll see to that.'

He was an altar-boy when he was at school, and he always had a word with Father Loney at the church door after Sunday Mass. He had more than a word this time.

'Mick Nolan?' said Father Loney. 'I know where the Nolans live. But I never see any of them at Mass.'

'But you'll try to persuade him, won't you, Father?' Terry pleaded 'To do the right thing.'

'The right thing,' said Father Loney, his hands deep in his soutane, his eyes looking down at his boots. 'Now that's the problem, Terry. A forced marriage often makes bad worse. But I'll see what I can do.'

Terry was disappointed that even a priest seemed unconcerned about the shame of an unmarried mother, but the Irish accent gave him a strange comfort. It carried the music of the Church he trusted, and he waited hopefully for the result of Father Loney's visit to the Nolans.

When he called at the house Father Loney found Mick's parents weren't interested. They said it was up to their son. Let him speak for himself. He did. Young Mick from Tordoch grinned at the old priest from Cork.

'Me? Get married? At my age! You kiddin?'

So Terry himself went to the house. Mrs Nolan answered the bell, flustered when she saw who it was.

'Away you go!' she bawled, a big-bosomed indignant woman. 'Don't you dare come here pestering decent folk … Haw, Paddy!'

Mr Nolan, an unemployed unshaven labourer in his shirtsleeves, came obediently to the door. With his wrists on his hips he hitched up his baggy trousers.

'What's up, Bridie?'

He sounded aggressive as he stood loyally behind his massive wife and gaped round her shoulder.

'This thing here,' said Mrs Nolan.

Terry saw the daughter of the house sidle into the lobby and peep at him curiously behind her parents. She gave him a little smile that distracted him for a moment. He had never spoken to her, though he knew she was Angela's age and her name was Teresa. She was a chubby plain-faced girl with thick legs. He ignored her and spoke stiffly to the mother.

'Am I to take it your son Michael is afraid to see me?' Mrs Nolan slammed the door.

But to Terry nothing was too much in Angela's cause. He stopped going to the library, went out every night, walked around, stood about, kept looking. It was the end of January before he caught up on his prey. He saw him coming out of the betting-shop beside the Tordoch Tavern, accosted him politely, and asked him what he was going to do about Angela.

Mick smiled, and stuffed a fistful of paper money into his pocket.

'Nothing,' he said.

'I see,' said Terry. 'In that case it's up to me to do something.'

A couple of Mick's friends coming from the betting-shop at his heels stopped to watch the encounter. They saw a slim youth, pale-faced and spectacled, trying to obstruct a reckless big-fisted fellow they knew was dangerous to cross. It was a sparrow challenging a hawk, and Terry was so solemn he looked ridiculous. It made them laugh.

'What do you mean, do something?' Mick jeered. 'An affiliation order? You got some hopes! Just try it, and I'll say I wasn't the only one.'

'But that's not true.'

'Maybe no. But I've got lotsa pals'll swear it is. They'll say your wee sister was easy.'

Terry shuddered. He put his hand across his face to hide his tears. He wanted to murder Mick Nolan. But he knew he would only make a fool of himself if he started a punch-up.

And he knew Mick had handers used to perjury. Any three of them were always on call to give false evidence if any two of them were charged with mugging a drunk old man. He knew them all, and knew what they were like. He had been at school with them. They had nearly sucked him into their whirlpool, till their language and way of life offended him. They provoked him to swim off on his own, to go to further education classes and get the job he was in.

He walked away. He knew he was beaten. There was nothing he could do to make Mick Nolan marry Angela.

He didn't tell his mother or sister what Mick had said, it hurt him too much. It was an insult to him as well as a slur on Angela. He couldn't let it go at that. The wound festered. Day and night he fretted for revenge.

It didn't take him long to see there was something he could try. He was on a bus in Cathedral Street when he saw Teresa Nolan coming out of Collins's at the end of her day's work. He noted the time, and as if by accident he met her there the next night.

She smiled when she saw him. It was a happy smile that made a dull face bright. He stopped, and spoke to her like an old friend.

'Hullo, Teresa! Nice to see you! We should be getting related. But Mick won't have it.'

'Oh, him!' she answered, just as friendly. 'You know what he's like.'

'Yes, I know,' he said, giving smile for smile. 'But never mind him! How about you? What are you doing tomorrow night, Teresa?'

She was flattered to be asked. She met him once a week to start with, then it was twice. Soon it was every other night, and she sang to herself at work and at home, she was so happy. She had never had a boy-friend before. She told her work-mates about him. One of them was her cousin, Bernadette Maloney. Bernadette had been in Terry's class in the primary school. She said he was snooty. Teresa said he wasn't. He was such a nice boy, with such nice manners, and such a wonderful lover, even if he did wear glasses, she was crazy about him. All the girls teased her, but she knew they were just envious. They were never done complaining about their boyfriends. None of them ever lasted more than a month or two, and it was always some jobless youth, coarse and unfaithful.

It irked her Terry insisted they mustn't meet locally.

'We don't want Mick to know,' he said.

'Why not?' said she, huffing.

'He doesn't like me. He would say I'm not good for you.'

'Oh, but you are!'

She hugged him in the darkness of a cranny in a waste-land far from home, her skirt up to her hips. She writhed and panted.

'Oh, don't! Please! Oh, I love it!'

'Of course, you do,' he said, and went on.

He roused himself as well as her. It was all so quick and easy, so acceptably repeated, and she was always so grateful, he wondered if that was how it had been for Angela. The speculation hardened his will to get even with Mick Nolan.

By the time the April showers stopped falling on the ruined city Teresa's condition was obvious to her parents. She told them who was to blame, and they sent Mick out to claim the culprit.

Terry was ready for him.

'It needn't be me,' he said. 'Could be anybody. Your sister, she's easy. Like you said about mine.'

Mick bunched his fists, opened them, and tried again.

'Aye, I know what I said. But I've got handers will swear what I tell them. You haven't.'

'You think not?' said Terry. 'Well, I can tell you something. Danny has made some good friends inside. Real hard men. Harder than you. Two of them have been

out since Christmas. They'll swear your Teresa was soft
if I tell Danny to fix them.'

'You bastard!' said Mick.

'Not me,' said Terry. 'You. You started it.'

Mick might have settled for a draw, but he was under
orders. His parents wanted Teresa married to Terry.

'He's got a rare job, that fella,' said Mrs Nolan. 'Teresa
could do a damn sight worse.'

'She's done better than I ever expected,' said Mr Nolan.

'You talk to him again, Mick,' said Mrs Nolan. 'They
say he's a decent enough lad. Even if he is a bit stuck-up.
Tell him he ought to do the right thing.'

'I'll try,' said Mick.

'What's more,' said Mrs Nolan, 'he's a good Catholic.
So we won't have any mixed-marriage trouble.'

'Don't tell me that's bothering you,' said Mr Nolan.

'Of course it is,' said Mrs Nolan. 'I want to see the girl
properly married.'

Mick went back to Terry. He kept it peaceful. He knew
that even if he hammered Terry, or got two strangers to
beat him up, it wouldn't guarantee a wedding. And he was
more amused than annoyed at what Terry had done to get
back at him.

'I didn't think you had that much spunk in you,' he said
with a grin.

They drank together in the Tordoch Tavern for an
hour. Terry was firm. He said marriage had no place in
his plans for the future. They kept going over it, drinking
halfs and half-pints till they were both unsteady. Mick put
his arm round Terry's shoulder, wheedling, man to man.

'Tell you what I'll do then,' he said. 'I'll marry Angela
if you'll marry Teresa.'

'You're getting the better bargain,' said Terry.

'Don't know about that,' said Mick. 'Teresa's good
about the house. You can make a right skivvy of her and
she'll never complain. But your Angela, no!'

Terry leaned over the bar, moved his glass round and round in widening circles. He had done all he set out to do. He had got even with Mick Nolan. Now the price frightened him.

'Come on!' said Mick. 'What the hell! It doesn't mean we can never have other women. We're young yet, you and me.'

'That's true,' said Terry.

There was a reception in the Miners' Welfare after the double wedding. Mick's parents and all his handers were there, and Teresa's friends from Collins's, making a convivial company, but Terry and Angela had only their mother. Mr Maloney, Teresa's uncle, stood half-soused behind a table in a corner of the hall and acted as barman, serving canned ale and whisky free on request, paid for by the Nolans.

Terry's mother had brought a record-player and a dozen records of Irish songs. She played them all, and the guests enjoyed a rousing sing-song of the rebel ballads the Glasgow-Irish love to remember when they have drink taken on a social occasion.

Teresa's grandfather sat beside her, mumbling. He had come over from Ireland when he was nineteen. As an old man, and the only Irish-born person there, he felt he had a right to criticise the singers and the songs.

'All these folk,' he said sourly. 'They keep on singing about dying for Ireland, and there's not wan of them ever seen the bloody country.'

'But it's where we all come from, granda,' said Teresa. 'You can't say we're Scotch.'

'And I wouldn't say these people are Irish,' said her grandfather. 'Mongrel Glasgow, that's all they are.'

'Wheesht, granda!' said Teresa. 'Somebody might hear you.'

'Tordoch!' the old man growled. 'What a place! Used to be all unspoiled country here.'

He staggered off to have his glass refilled, and Teresa went over to sit beside Angela. Big-bellied, and flushed from the heat of the hall, they spoke shyly together, two sisters-in-law getting acquainted.

Terry weaved across from the bar with a full glass in his hand and tried to give them a smile. He couldn't quite manage it. He knew he had been drinking too much and he didn't feel real.

His mother lurched behind, clutched his elbow, and pulled him aside. The drink she had taken made her voice harsh.

'I told you before and I tell you again,' she said. 'You did a damn stupid thing.'

'I know,' said Terry.

'It's God's mercy poor wee Teresa Nolan's too simple to know why you did it. May she never find out!'

'She won't,' said Terry. 'Not from me. And Mick promised me he would never....'

'All those books you used to read,' said his mother. 'They made you think you were clever. You were going to rise in the world. But you're stuck here, as Irish as the rest of us.'

'I don't think so,' said Terry.

'You would have been far better doing nothing about Angela's trouble. Stupid old-fashioned ideas you had! Now she'll never get out of Tordoch. Nor will you.'

'Oh, but I will,' said Terry. 'And I'll take Teresa. If she'll come. If she can't or won't, I'll leave her.'

'Suppose you do get out,' said his mother. 'Angela will still be married to Mick Nolan. And you know what he'll be like. He'll batter her every Saturday night. You'll have to stand by to help her for the rest of your life.'

'I know,' said Terry. 'What else can I do? She's my sister.'

I'm Leaving You

They were both in their early thirties. They had no children, and their parents were dead. She was the daughter of a surgeon in the Royal Infirmary, and he was the son of a lawyer. When they were orphaned they each inherited a parental house and some six or seven thousand pounds. They had no brother or sister to share the legacies.

She was educated at Laurel Bank, and he had gone to Glasgow Academy. They met at the university. Their first date was the night he took her to the Rugby Club dance. After a wasted year he stopped idling with beer and billiards and scraped a degree in Economics the year she got an honours degree in French and German.

They married when he began to find his way in the world of business, and she did occasional teaching in her old school. She didn't want a regular job. She didn't mind staying at home. She managed to get a woman to come in once a week to do the rougher chores, but that was all. The rest she did herself, playing the part of a good wife who looked after the comforts of her husband.

He agreed she didn't need to work. They weren't rich, he said, but they weren't poor. By the time he was thirty he had a good post in a big imports-and-exports firm, with his own office and a secretary. They were living in a flat in Kersland Street, but they wanted out of it.

When her father died they sold his house in Giffnock

because it was on the wrong side of the river for them. But when his father died too they moved into his house in Bearsden. They liked the place. It had a two-car garage, and they could afford two cars. They thought it would be silly to sell another house just to put more money in the bank, and then go on living in a flat they didn't like.

They had been married seven years when it happened. He was dumb when she told him.

She came out with it one night in April after she had cleared away their evening meal. She marched from the kitchen to the sitting-room and thumped down on her chair. She kept staring at him as if her eyes could send a laser beam through his *Financial Times*.

Her penetrating silence made him peep over his paper. He never said much to her after their first couple of years together, and she never said much to him. Her silence shouldn't have disturbed him. But that night it came over as a demand to sit up and listen. He put his paper on his lap and looked at her patiently. He always paid her the courtesy of listening whenever she had a passing mood to talk to him.

The moment he put his paper down she spoke abruptly.

'I'm leaving you,' she said.

She wasn't smiling and she was quite calm. He couldn't take it as a joke or hysteria. It was a cold statement of fact.

He didn't know what to say or how to behave. He gaped at her, and waited. His reaction angered her. She spoke rather loudly.

'You're not the least bit bothered, are you? You sit there, and I might as well be telling you I'm going shopping in town tomorrow, for all you care.'

'That's not fair,' he said. 'It's just I don't understand. What do you mean, you're leaving me?'

'I mean I'm leaving you,' she repeated. 'Packing up and going.'

'But why on earth,' he started to ask.

He felt she was trying to be dramatic when their life hadn't a script with any drama in it.

'Because I'm fed up,' she said fiercely.

'I see,' he said. But he didn't.

'Is that all you've got to say?' she cried. 'But of course you never have anything to say, have you? My God, you're dull! Dull, dull, dull!'

'I'm sorry,' he said.

He was too shocked to say any more, and she was furious at his humility. She had expected him to make frantic appeals, to argue and fight about it, to be angry and try to talk her out of it. She was as baffled as he was.

He picked up his paper and used it as a shield against her till he thought of something to say. The idea that she would leave him was absurd, yet it terrified him. His retreat provoked her to another attack.

'I'm fed up living here,' she raised her voice again. 'And I'm fed up with you! Your laziness, and your selfishness. The way you sit there night after night and fall asleep on your chair. My God! I daren't contemplate life with you when you're middle-aged.'

'You'll be middle-aged too then,' he said behind his paper, very sour.

'My mind is made up,' she said. 'I'm going. In fact, my case is packed and in my car. I'm going tonight.'

'If that's what you want,' he said.

He saw no use arguing if her mind was made up. He wouldn't go on his knees to her and make a fool of himself.

'My God! Will nothing move you?' she screamed. 'Good God Almighty, are you made of wood?'

'I wish you'd leave God out of this,' he said.

'You sit there like a bloody turnip,' she said.

The remark hurt him. He knew he was putting on weight. He laughed it off by saying all rugby players put on weight when they gave up the game. But he thought it unkind of her to call him a turnip. Worse, a bloody turnip.

'There's no need to swear,' he said.

'You'd make a saint swear,' she retorted. 'A woman tells her husband she's leaving him, and the husband reads his paper and says all right, if that's what you want. What kind of a man are you?'

'I hope I'm too much of a gentleman ... ' he began to answer.

'Oh yes, always the gentleman, that's you!' she interrupted him. 'Never raises his voice or his hand to a woman. All manners and no matter.'

'I was going to say,' he continued, proud to be calm when she wasn't, 'I hope I'm too much of a gentleman to demand obedience from any woman. I respect you—'

'Thanks very much,' she said.

'I have never regarded you as my slave or my property,' he kept going.

'Aren't we noble!' she jeered.

She bounced out of her chair and walked round the room, pulling her fingers. His head swivelled to watch her as he went on talking.

'I've always respected the freedom of women. You know that. If you want to go, and your mind is made up, I can't stop you. You're a free person.'

'You mean I can go and you don't care?' she asked over her shoulder.

'That's not what I said,' he replied. 'I care very much. You've never given me any reason to think you felt this way. But what I feel, what I may suffer, doesn't concern you if your mind is made up.'

She went back to her chair and tried again to make him understand.

'I'm in a rut,' she said. 'I haven't had a holiday abroad since the day we were married. It has always been your fishing and golfing holidays. I'm fed up with it.'

'You've never complained,' he said.

'I'm complaining now,' she told him. 'It's eight years since I was last in Germany, and I've never been anywhere in Austria. The places I've never seen! I'm stuck here in this house all day, and there's not enough in it for an intelligent woman.'

'You could get a job if you want to,' he said.

'And look after you as well?' she challenged him. 'You want me to do two jobs?'

'Other women do two jobs,' he said.

'That's not the point,' she snapped. 'I want away from you, and that's all.'

'Well, if that's what you want,' he said again.

She nearly apologised before she left, as if at the last minute she felt she was treating him rather harshly. She said there didn't need to be anything final about it, she didn't want a divorce or anything like that. But she must have a change or she would go off her head. She would think about it again after a month or two. Then she told him she had got herself a job in a translation bureau, and she had arranged to share a service-flat with Shona McGregor. He was amazed at her duplicity in planning it all without ever giving him a word of warning.

'I'll get in touch,' she said. 'Not at once, of course. But later on. And we can discuss how it's working out.'

'Yes, that's fine,' he told her. 'We'll do that.'

When she left him he went about his work in a state of anesthesia. Nothing seemed quite real. He didn't sleep well.

He told nobody he was living a bachelor's life again, and he didn't think his wife would go around telling people she had left him because she was bored. Yet it was soon common knowledge. Perhaps he helped to make it so, for he was clumsy in deceit the first time he was asked about her. He was brooding over a drink at the bar before going for lunch in the Malmaison when he was slapped

hard on the shoulder. He turned irritably. It was Bob
Ramsay, a genial fellow who was scrum-half with him for
a season in the university fifteen.

'Hullo there!' he welcomed the intruder.

'Hiya, Jack?' said Ramsay with a grin of manly
affection. 'Long time no see, eh?'

They shook hands, agreed it was over a year since they
met. When their chat rambled on they bought each other
a drink, and then another drink.

'And how's Jean these days?' Ramsay asked at the
fag-end of their conversation.

'Oh, Jean?' he said cautiously. 'Well now—Jean—she's
gone to her mother for a week or two. Just for a change
of air, you know. She's been off colour lately.'

Ramsay frowned at the limp falsehood.

'Back to her mother? I thought her mother was dead.'

'Oh God, so she is!' said Jack. 'That's right. I forgot.'

He splayed his fingertips across his temple, his elbow
on the bar. He had meant to have one short drink only
before lunch, and now he was on his fourth. It wasn't that
he couldn't carry his liquor, but it was the wrong time of
day. He felt silly.

Ramsay squeezed his arm, shook it gently.

'Come on now,' he wheedled. 'Tell the truth. You're
not looking yourself at all, Jack. You've lost weight.
What's going on? Tell me.'

Jack told him.

'I know what's the matter with her,' said Ramsay.

'Yes?' said Jack.

He was eager to listen to anybody who would talk
about Jean.

'She's had things too damned easy,' said Ramsay.
'You've been too soft with her. If she had a couple of kids
to look after, and no money of her own, she wouldn't act
so high and mighty. She's a spoiled girl. Always was. Too
much money behind her.'

'Money has nothing to do with it,' said Jack. 'Jean and I were never hard-up, but we were never well-off.'

'That's what you think,' said Ramsay.

'She was never a spoiled girl with me,' said Jack. 'There was nothing she wouldn't do for me.'

'Except live with you,' said Ramsay.

'Well, that's the problem, isn't it?' said Jack. 'It doesn't make sense. I never expected it. I can't think what came over her.'

'You take my Kath,' said Ramsay. He too was affected by extra drinks at midday, and he spoke with foolish pride. 'That girl didn't bring me a penny when I married her. And you know the old man left me a lot less than I thought he had. So Kath goes out to work mornings in a prep school and looks after me and our wee girl and runs the house, and she's too busy to be bored.'

'Good for her,' said Jack.

'Yes, she's a good woman, my Kath,' said Ramsay. 'We pull together.'

'Good for you,' said Jack, but it was more of a snub than a compliment.

'All right,' Ramsay apologised. 'I always say the wrong things, don't I? I'm sorry, Jack. But I do feel for you.'

He wanted to help. He told Jack there was no point going about looking miserable and feeling sorry for himself. He coaxed him to come to a club where four or five old rugby players met every Friday night for a drinking-session. He said they often spoke of him. They still remembered the great try he scored after a forty yards run when he played in a select fifteen against the London Scottish.

The welcome he got when Ramsay took him there was like the kiss of life to a man rescued from drowning. He moved from the dark of loneliness to the light of company. His memorable try was mentioned in the course of the evening and he felt he was a person of some standing among old friends.

He went back fuddled to his empty house. Somewhere in a bureau-bookcase there was an envelope with presscuttings from *The Scotsman* and the *Herald*. His reborn ego was confirmed when he read again the report that said his try against the London Scottish was 'a thrilling performance'.

'And she called me dull!' he said, swaying. 'Me? Dull? It's not me, it's her.'

His moping days were over. He began to look at the many girls the firm employed. It was, he believed, a purely aesthetic interest in the walk and figure of certain females. Then his secretary went away to look after an ailing father. He was given the smartest girl in the typing-pool as a stand-in. She was young and pretty, and she became very congenial to him. From the way she always hovered at the door before she would leave him, the way she looked at him tenderly, he guessed she knew his wife had left him. Her fond young eyes were silently saying she was sorry for the wrong done to him.

She wasn't the only one who made him feel better. All the girls went out of their way to be nice to him. It gave him a twisted amusement to see people being sorry for him when he was trying to stop being sorry for himself.

He was coping quietly with his new life when a senior colleague's secretary left to get married. It was a surprise. She had been with the firm for years, and she was turned thirty. Nobody ever thought she had a life outside the office. And because she had given such long and excellent service there was an office party and a wedding presentation, with plenty of drink and a buffet. He was stuck in a corner most of the time with one girl after another.

His temporary secretary came very close, shoulder to shoulder, thigh against thigh. He cuddled her discreetly, his hand squeezing her waist, then under her arm to fondle a breast. She was flushed with sherry followed by gin, and he was carefree with whisky.

The incident made him ambitious, but he didn't start an affair until his new secretary came. She was a beautiful slim brunette, efficient and attentive. He meant nothing by it when, looking at the *Herald* over mid-morning coffee, he remarked there seemed to be a lot of hotels opening round about the city. She read the full-page advert he showed her, and commented on the picture of the luxurious lounge-bar and the dining room.

'Looks super,' she said. 'I do love a drink and a meal in a place like that.'

To prove he wasn't so dull that he couldn't take a hint he asked her to go there with him and see how the reality compared with the advert.

He behaved very prudently when he took her out. He was no excited schoolboy, he kept telling himself. He could wait and see. He didn't even attempt a good-night kiss when they parted. It was three weeks before he took her at the end of an evening to the bleak house where he lived alone. He started to explain once more about his wife, but she said it didn't matter. She had heard it all already, and she wasn't bothered.

'It's her own fault if you—' she said, and stopped.

'A man like you needs a woman,' she tried again.

She made it easy for him, but he didn't often take her into his house overnight. He didn't think it wise to get involved with a woman working in the same firm, and he had no complaints when, as calmly as she started the liaison, she told him it would have to end. The man she was engaged to marry was coming home from an eight months tour of duty with an oil company in the Middle East. She had never mentioned any man before. He was surprised again how secretive women could be when it suited them.

'I was just as lonely as you' she explained. 'But I didn't

want to say I was engaged in case it sort of inhibited you.
You're so moral really. Still, I think we helped each other
through a difficult time.'

'Yes, indeed,' he said.

'I don't think I took more than I gave,' she said.

'Oh no,' he said.

When it was all over he was left with a feeling of
gratitude rather than affection, and with that experience
behind him he was confident he could find another
woman whenever he liked.

But he didn't particularly want to start another affair.
He drifted back to his bachelor's habits. Every week he
had at least one drinking-session with Ramsay and others.
Sometimes two or three of them went out on a pub-crawl
for the sake of variety, wearing an old suit and raincoat.

There was a touch of daring in it, a quest for adventure.
They drank pints from the city centre to the south side or
east end, trying pubs that catered for queer types or rough
customers.

They knew it was madness, but they enjoyed their
pub-crawls and made them a weekly habit.

On those nights he left his car at home and travelled by
bus. He was very strict about not driving when he had
been drinking. And it was on one of those nights that Jean
saw him from her car when he was waiting for a bus home.
She was held up at the lights, and there he was, loitering
at the kerb.

If he had gone to the bus station she wouldn't have seen
him, but his company broke up at a corner where it was
easier for him to walk on to the next stop than to go a
long way back to the terminus where the Bearsden bus
came in. He was so confused after an evening's heavy
drinking that he didn't notice he was waiting at a
Corporation bus stop instead of the stop for a country
bus.

When the lights changed Jean reacted quickly. She

made a left hand turn into a sidestreet, left her car smartly, locked the door, and hurried back. She was unhappy at what she had seen. He was rocking there blind to the world, round-shouldered and talking to himself. He looked wretched and neglected.

'What's he standing there for?' she wondered as she ran. 'And that old coat! I could have sworn I gave it away to a jumble sale. My God, he had let himself go. Oh, the fool! And why hasn't he his car?'

She was unhappy enough before she saw him. She was on her way back from Pollokshaws after a visit to an old girlfriend who had a husband and two little boys. Her visit was a flop. The husband disappeared five minutes after she arrived, as if she was a bore he couldn't be expected to endure. And the two little boys clamoured so much for attention that her conversation with their mother was a series of interruptions. She didn't like it. She saw it as proof that even from childhood the male insists on women giving him priority.

She was still in a bad mood on her way back to her service-flat, and she wasn't comforted to think what she would have to put up with when she got there. Shona McGregor never stopped talking, and she always had to have the radio or television on. It had given her a recurrent headache over the months, and she longed for some domestic peace and quiet. She missed her own corner and the chance to sit down with a book.

Jack was still rocking at the bus stop when she came running round the corner.

'What are you doing here?' she demanded, very strict with him.

'Waiting for a bus,' he said.

He didn't say it as a rude answer to a daft question. He was, as always, polite. He said it with a smile, patiently explaining what might not be obvious, even to a person of her intelligence.

'You're drunk,' she said.

'Not me,' he said, and raised a palm in protest.

'And you need a shave,' she said.

He rubbed his chin with trembling fingers.

'You could be right,' he said.

'Where's your car?' she asked.

'Car?' he said. 'Oh yes, car. Well, you see—'

He couldn't think. She was so severe she frightened him. He saw his drinking-sessions banned, his next affair stopped before it started, and an end to his free and easy hours of coming and going when he pleased.

'I've been phoning you every night for the past month,' she said. 'You're never in.'

'That's right,' he mumbled. 'I'm always out.'

'Oh, stop your nonsense,' she said. 'It's time you—'

'Here's my bus,' he interrupted her, and moved from the kerb to the road, his arm up in a signal.

'That's not your bus!' she called after him. 'That's a Corporation bus.'

He was on it and away, and he raised a hand in a parting salute from the platform.

She ran back to her car. She would drive on at speed and be home before him. He would have a long walk after he left the Corporation bus. She would go in and wait for him and talk frankly. Then she wasn't so sure.

'What if he's not going straight home?' she faltered as she doubled back to the main road. 'And that's why he took that bus. But then, where can he be going at this time of night?'

She drove on, arguing with herself.

'It doesn't matter,' she said in the end. 'He must come in sooner or later. And I'll be there. I'm going back home, back to my own house and my own things, and I'll wait for him. And I'll tell him something. I'll shake him.'

It was only then she remembered that when she left she had forgotten to take her key.

Quoth The Budgie

It was half-past ten at night in the peaceful house of an
elderly schoolmaster and his childless wife. She was talking
to her budgie, and he was reading. He looked up and
complained.

'You pay more attention to that thing than to me.'

He got a sharp reply. 'At least he answers me when I
speak to him.'

They sometimes pretended to be cross with each other,
to put some variety into a quiet life. But they were never
in danger of a real quarrel.

So she went on talking to her budgie. It was in a big
cage, mounted on a chromium shaft nearly as tall as
herself, and the tiny bird answered obscurely now and
again.

Mr Green returned to his book. He was getting a bit
soured at the way his wife kept fussing over her pet. But
he always tried to be patient with her faults. And after
thirty years of uneventful married life, it would be absurd
to start quarrelling with her over a silly bird.

She talked so much he couldn't go on reading. He put
his book down and looked at her. He would never tell her,
but it pleased him to see she had kept her figure, though
her hair was going grey. She was still smart and graceful,
and she had been his cheerful slave since the day they were
married.

But now inside his bald head a crabbit voice was saying things he would never have said aloud.

'Stupid woman! Baby-talk to a bloody budgie!'

His wife took leave of the bird as if leaving a friend.

'Good night, Riki.'

The bird squawked an echo.

'Night kee-kee!'

She wouldn't take that for an answer.

'No, no! It's you that's Riki. I'm Nan.'

She tried again.

'You say, good night Nan. Good night Nan.'

The bird tried again.

'Night-nan.'

She put the black cloth over the cage and lilted her words.

'See you in the morning!'

Riki protested in a flurry of squeaks with the same rhythm.

Nan turned to her husband, eager to have him share her delight.

'Did you hear that? Riki said what I said! See you in the morning!'

She went upstairs, and when he was sure she was in bed reading her woman's weekly for half-an-hour before she put the light out, he opened the sideboard quietly and hauled out his bottle of whisky. He poured a dram, sat down to work at the desk of his bureau-bookcase, and stayed up drinking till one in the morning.

He was trying to compile a book of verse for use in schools. He had been vexed when a young colleague published a textbook on the new maths. He himself, twice as old, and head of his department, with an honours degree in English, had nothing to his name. He wanted to do something about it, and show a young teacher that an old man too could get a textbook published. And so he began collecting poems, and when from time to time his wife asked what he was doing, sitting up so late, he told her.

'I'm working on my anthology.'

He wasn't making much progress. He muttered to the papers on his desk.

'It's a pity Nan's no help to me here. She's a good housewife, but she's not very bright. Poor nan!'

Upstairs in bed, poor Nan wasn't feeling well. She had a sudden pain when she put the light out. She couldn't understand it, and it wouldn't go away. When she rose in the morning she looked so ill, that Mr Green told her to go back to bed. Dumb and suffering, she did what she was told.

When he came home that evening, she was up and dressed, talking to her budgie. She turned to greet him, flushed with excitement.

'He was talking away to me there like billy-o! Isn't that right, Riki? You're my pal!'

Riki agreed at once.

'My pal.'

She gave the bird a dopey smile. Mr Green was annoyed. he spoke to her severely.

'You should be in your bed. You don't look well.'

She tottered to the edge of a chair and answered weakly.

'I think you're right. I don't feel well.'

But she wouldn't go back to bed till she had served him his evening meal and washed up after it. And even then she put it off for an hour, chatting to Riki. She stood beside the cage like a teacher encouraging a backward child to read, saying the same words over and over again till he could repeat them.

She crumbled a fragment of a tea-biscuit on a spoon, and moistened the crumbs with a drop of cold tea before she fed him. When he finished, there were crumbs on his beak. She wiped them off with a paper hanky and scolded him.

'Dirty face!'

Riki bounced back.

'Dirty face!'

She wagged a finger at him.

'That's all! You're getting no more.'

Riki flapped, and squawked.

'No more!'

Mr Green lost patience with the pair of them. He spoke roughly.

'Come on! Get to your bed, Nan!'

With a quick echo, Riki squawked at him.

'Bed-nan.'

Nan laughed as she covered the cage, but it was the twisted laugh of a sick woman.

Mr Green told her to go and see the doctor in the morning. She tried to argue.

'Wait around in that surgery, with all those folk the picture of misery. Not me! I hate that place!'

He insisted, and she obeyed. She always did what he told her. But she had great satisfaction in telling him about her visit.

'A waste of time! I think he thinks there's nothing wrong with me. Or if there is, he doesn't know what. Stay in bed for a couple of days, says he. I can just see me!'

She made little of the days when her pain was bad, and made a lot of the days when she was feeling fine. But the pain came back more and more often, and one morning she had to stay in bed in spite of herself. She wasn't fit to get up and go to the doctor. The doctor had to come to her. He was puzzled when he came downstairs, and asked Mr Green if she had had an accident recently, a fall of some kind, or knocked her head against anything.

She had fallen downstairs a month ago, Mr Green remembered. But she hadn't hurt herself. He ran at once when he heard her scream, and she said she was all right. The doctor shook his head sadly, and said he would call again tomorrow.

Nan submitted to her illness as meekly as she submitted to her husband. She was more concerned about Riki than about herself. Mr Green was less concerned about either of them than about his own troubles. He stayed off school for two days to attend to his wife, but he couldn't go on doing that. He got a woman to come in, from ten in the morning till late afternoon, to look after her.

Nan wanted Riki brought up to her bedroom, but the doctor said no. Lying there all day with the bird for company she would only tire herself talking too much. She must have rest and quiet,and try to sleep.

Before she would agree Riki would have to stay downstairs she pleaded to have him up beside her for an hour. They spoke together, with Mr Green hovering around, and at the end of their dialogue she gave the bird her final instructions.

'If they're not good to you, you tell Nan. Mind! Tell Nan.'

She told the daily help what to do about the budgie, and told her husband where to buy the right packets of seed, and she said he must let the bird out of its cage for a while every day.

He was surprised. He had never seen it out of its cage.

As if admitting a guilty secret she explained. She let it out when he was away all day, because she knew he wouldn't like it flying round the room when he was reading.

Putting himself out in the morning with a slice of toast and marmalade, he missed the good breakfasts he used to get. And coming home in the evening to a cold collation left in the fridge by the daily help, or sometimes trying to make a hot meal for himself, he behaved with the dignity of a brave man who knows he is unjustly punished by cruel circumstance.

He was used to the comfort of seeing his wife coming

and going about his house in perfect health. He was used to the pleasure she brought him when she entered a room, so mild and calm her accustomed presence. Her illness offended him.

When he went upstairs to ask her how she was feeling she answered vaguely, and asked how Riki was doing. She worried about him.

'He must be missing me. He needs someone to talk to. Do try and talk to him, won't you? Please!'

He promised, but he was beginning to hate a creature he had never liked. He was hot and bothered every time he opened the cage. He watched the bird nervously when it flew round the room, perched on top of the bureau-bookcase, when it went over and under its cage but wouldn't go in. He was never at ease till it was back inside, and he had the cage closed. And when he sat down at last to his whisky and his anthology he cried aloud in vexation.

'That bloody bird! It's more trouble than she is.'

For Nan gave him no trouble. When he asked if there was anything she wanted she always said no. And he didn't bother her much. He took a sullen pride in coping unaided.

But he soon wearied of his self-service. There seemed no end to it. It was only what he feared when the doctor said she would have to be moved. The thought of her in hospital depressed him, but Nan seemed past caring.

Left alone with Riki he thought of selling the bird. He hadn't the heart to destroy it. But since he hoped Nan would soon be home again, he didn't dare get rid of it behind her back. Then, in his loneliness, he got into the habit of speaking to it as he had been told to do. Sometimes he spoke in exasperation. He had no patience when it answered him in a screechy mimicry of what he said, and he often lost his temper with it.

He was sitting drinking in the small hours, still trying

to arrange the poems in his anthology and decide what to keep in and what to leave out, when the bird suddenly spoke to him. He couldn't make out the words, and he turned on it peevishly.

'Shut up, you yellow basket!'

Riki fluttered to the top of his ladder, flounced there in a bad temper, and gave back the insult.

'Ya yella basket.'

He came down again, still flapping. He made angry little noises, and his chest went out in defiance. He looked fierce. With his beak through the cage he threatened clearly.

'I'll tell Nan.'

Mr Green rose, shaking his fist, his voice raised.

'You'll tell Nan? I'm the one that'll tell Nan! I'll tell her what you are—you're a little pest!'

The moment the words were out of his mouth, he was shocked at himself.

'What the hell am I doing? Arguing with a brainless bird! What a stupid thing to say—I'm the one that'll tell Nan.'

He didn't get the chance to tell Nan anything. His visits to the hospital were an ordeal. Soon they were pointless. She lay in a trance, grey and mute. The death certificate said she died of a cerebral tumour.

He was less fit for living alone than he thought he would be. He began to drink more every night, starting earlier and finishing later. Even so, his sleep was broken. He went to the doctor and asked for sleeping pills.

His days were heavy with grief, and the unwanted legacy of Riki was only a nuisance. But he still hadn't the heart to sell or destroy the bird. He knew Nan wouldn't like it, and although she was gone for ever he had a persistent feeling, a faith or a hope, that she lived on somewhere and saw all he did, and knew even his most secret thoughts. So whenever the bird was silent for a long spell he spoke to it gently for her sake. Sometimes, when it spoke without his encouragement, he felt it was really talking to Nan in a private dialogue, where all he was allowed to hear was what the bird said. He was frightened by the thought of a pet bird conversing with a dead woman.

He broke down completely one midnight in December. To comfort his loneliness he often spoke aloud, and now he chatted to Nan as if she were still there. He asked her to come and talk to Riki. He raised his voice. he knew he had to shout to make her hear, she was so far away. And he badly wanted her help, for he had no conversation for a bird, or for anybody.

The loud voice excited Riki. He screeched his own appeals, and in spasms of chatter he repeated all the phrases Nan had ever taught him. he stopped as abruptly as he had started, and peered through his cage.

The sad look in the little eyes made Mr Green remember he hadn't opened the cage for a couple of days. He apologised to the pining bird, and released it. He watched it fly across the room in short flights, perching here and there for a moment. Then it soared to the top of the bureau-bookcase, and settled there on a small bust of Milton Mr Green had bought in a junk shop years ago. From that height it looked curiously down on the drunk man.

A sudden rustling in the curtains startled Mr Green. But it was only the wind coming through a window not properly closed. That, and nothing more. He turned and stared at the silent bird. Its beak went tapping gently on the shoulder of the bust. Mr Green screamed.

'Stop that!'

The bird glared, grim and ominous.

Mr Green raised an accusing finger and staggered as he ranted.

'I know who you are! I cut you out of my anthology!

The fowl whose fiery eyes.... Once upon a midnight dreary....'

Riki didn't answer, and Mr Green lurched away. He poured another whisky, and before he put the bottle down he held it up to the light. There wasn't much left. He pondered, weak and weary, then decided.

'I've had a lot tonight. I'll take no more.'

Riki echoed him, lamenting.

'No more Nan. Bed Nan. No more.'

Mr Green looked up at the bird again. He remembered the night he had seen Nan feed it with moistened crumbs, and then wipe its beak. He spoke to it viciously.

'Dirty face! That's what Nan called you. And you know what I called you? A little pest—you're a little pest.'

He swayed, clicked his fingers at the bird, and whispered kindly.

'You miss Nan? She was my pal. I miss Nan.'

Stately on Milton's head Riki counter-claimed.

'My pal.'

Mr Green knew his grief would never end so long as this unreasonable creature went on evoking the woman who was gone. He waved his hands at the bookcase, trying to get the bird to come down.

'Come on now! Back into your cage. I'll tell you what I'll do.'

Riki obeyed him in its own good time.

Mr Green started again.

'I'll tell you what. We'll both go and see Nan. You can tell Nan and I'll tell Nan. What do you think of that? Only, you go first.'

He moved with care to carry out his plan. He crumbled three sleeping pills on a dessert spoon and damped them with a generous drop of whisky. Through the door of the cage he offered the mixture.

Riki took it with grave and stern decorum. He sagged when the spoon was empty, gawked, and dropped to the floor.

Mr Green went upstairs to the bathroom, put into a glass of water all the pills he had left and gulped them down. Then he drank the rest of his whisky, went into the bedroom and lay down in the dark.

A Couple Of Old Bigots

The two miners reached the place together and Geddes lay down on the pavement. He grunted, resigned to his daily darg. Crouched on his side in an inch of water he prepared to start hewing.

'How now,' he declaimed, 'which of your hips has the most profound sciatica?'

He wriggled from his hip to his back, the pick under his right hand. Self-educated beyond his station, he liked to come out with the odd bits of Shakespeare he had learnt by heart and he got a kick out of throwing to Liam Rooney, his neighbour at the coal-face, the scraps of his unguided reading. Sometimes he did it from simple generosity, sometimes from malice aforethought. He was a quarrelsome atheist, and baiting Rooney, a practising Catholic, kept him happy. They were the best of friends.

'Tell me this, Liam,' he heaved through his toiling. 'Do you believe in free will?'

'I wish you'd give your tongue a wee rest,' Rooney complained, pushing the hutch nearer. 'You're aye blethering a lot of bloody nonsense.'

'No, but do you?' Geddes persisted. 'Damn it all, man, you surely ken what you're supposed to believe.'

'Ay, all right then, I believe in free will,' Rooney conceded. He thought the best policy was to humour Geddes, to be a willing victim and let him have his joke and his triumph. But sometimes he wished he could find an answer that Geddes couldn't use. When that ambition came to him he would make up his mind to read a book, but he never found the time and he never found the book.

'And do you believe God's almighty?' Geddes pursued him with a negroid grin.

'Of course He is,' Rooney answered impatiently. He knew there was a trap being sprung, but he couldn't see how to avoid it. 'How could He be God if He's no'?'

'But he canny be, no' if every man's got free will,' Geddes gloated up at him. 'Ye canny have it baith ways.'

'Whit way can I no'?' Rooney demanded.

Geddes kept it up, but it led nowhere. At the end of the shift they left the place together and walked one behind the other the couple of miles to the cage. They were working at the furthest point from the main road and lagged a fair distance behind the other miners. Then Geddes stopped suddenly, his hand out to stop Rooney too. They heard a creaking in the pine props, but they weren't sure where it came from.

'Go on!' Rooney screamed, pushing Geddes forward.

'No, get back,' Geddes shouted, shoving Rooney the other way.

The speed of his turn threw him off balance and he finished up sprawling across Rooney just as the first of the fall came down. It cut them off from the rest of the shift, and it was all over in less than a minute. The tumult was like a tenement collapsing, like thunder directly overhead.

'Jesus, Mary and Joseph!' Rooney panted, blessing himself. He gawked up at the threatening roof. The roar of its anger stopped, and there was only an occasional belch as some fragments shifted, a mild pattering as the soil filtered through.

'I wonder how long that's been pickling,' Geddes muttered resentfully. 'They ought to have kent aboot that.'

Rooney squatted on his hunkers, gulping and mouthing. He wanted to speak, to ask questions that Geddes would answer encouragingly since Geddes was the clever one with an answer to everything, but he couldn't get a word out.

'How much of it fell do you think?' Geddes asked him.

'A hell of a lot by the sound of it,' Rooney whispered, really frightened.

They were three and a half days in there together and stuck it out well because they were old friends, though Rooney lost his temper twice. The first time was when Geddes laughed at him for taking out his rosary and saying Our Fathers and Hail Marys on and on, mysteriously.

'Christ, dae ye aye carry thae beads wi' ye?' he scoffed.

'Ye ken damn fine I aye have my rosary in my pocket,' Rooney snapped. 'And ye could do worse than say a wee prayer yourself.'

The second time he lost his temper was half-way through the second day when Geddes was seized with a sudden spasm of vigour and hammed too near the bone.

'Ay, but to die, and go we know not where,
To lie in cold obstruction and to rot.'

'Ach, shut yer face,' Rooney growled. 'We're no' a' that deid yet.'

To begin with they did what they could to clear away the rubble, cheering each other, keeping their spirits up with guessing-games, football quizzes and songs. Geddes sang 'The Star o' Rabbie Burns' and Rooney taught him 'Faith of Our Fathers'. They drank the moisture that dripped from the roof, but long before they were rescued they were too weak to move. They were silent for hours at a stretch, past singing and arguing. The knocking they had answered over the nightmare term of darkness came slowly nearer and they sat against the wall and waited.

'Are ye all right, Liam?' Geddes croaked.

'Ay, I'm grand, Willie,' Rooney breathed faintly.

'It'll no be lang noo,' Geddes comforted him. 'Ay, we'll be having a pint in Sloan's the morrow night, you and me, so we will.'

The first small gap appeared. They heard voices come through loud and clear. They got a glimpse of Lumsden, the brusher, and the wall-eye of Grant the drawer. Then a large anonymous hand came to them with food and drink.

It wasn't the first accident they were in, and it wasn't the last, but it was the only time they were alone together. It was one more bond between them. They went back to work on the same day, still neighbours on the same shift, and their dialogue went on as before.

'Willie Geddes has got some terrible stories about the Popes, Rooney told his wife. 'I don't know where he gets the half of them. But if he's right there's been some quare old birds in the Vatican.'

'Sure everybody knows there's been bad Popes,' Mrs Rooney shrugged it off, ladling out his soup. 'You don't need Willie Geddes to tell you that.'

'Well, he's told me one or two things I never knew,' Rooney said grudgingly. 'Then he says, Ay, and you believe the Pope's infallible!'

His daughter looked up perkily from her secondary school homework spread out at the other end of the kitchen table and gave him advice.

'Just you tell him the Church doesn't say the Pope's impeccable.'

Her father glowered at her, ready to be embarrassed by the implications of the strange word. She explained it.

'Jees, I'll catch him with that one tomorrow,' he laughed. 'That's a rare word that is.'

The next time Geddes got on to the lives of the Popes Rooney carefully repeated what his daughter told him.

'Have you been reading a book?' Geddes asked sourly.

'Och, I don't need to be reading books,' Rooney joked. 'I learned a thing or two at school. Of course an Orangeman like you canny understand Catholic doctrine.'

'I'm no' an Orangeman,' Geddes shouted, angry at the name. 'I read the Freethinker every week, as you damn well know.'

'Well you ought to be,' Rooney cut back at him. 'Sure your father was, and his father afore him.'

'Keep my father out of it,' Geddes huffed. 'I know a lot mair aboot religion than a bigot like you.'

'I'm no' a bigot,' Rooney protested. 'It's you that's the bigot.'

'It's no', it's you,' Geddes insisted. 'You'll never admit you're in the wrong.'

'I will so, if I am,' Rooney retorted. It's you that's always sure you're right.'

It went on like that for years, and as they spent their days in familiar disputation old age came along and joined them, making in their company a third of whose presence they were only slowly aware. They became old grey men, they qualified for their pension, they stopped working, they mooned about the dying mining village, they drank together in Sloan's, and Geddes always got on to religion. The retreating years were making Rooney more devout, and more touchy in his piety, but they were making Geddes more aggressive, as if he had to prove his case to Rooney before it was too late and death proved everything.

They were two dottering old men, two local worthies, and the village smiled on their crabbit friendship and loved them equally. They might have gone to their common end still friends if Geddes hadn't said too much in Sloan's one Saturday night with a good drink on him. He dragged in the Virgin Mary and spoke of her with a coarseness he had never used before. He had been clever

and sarcastic, he had been jocular and irreverent, but
never coarse. Rooney was shocked. He was hurt. He
looked into his pint and shook his head over it.

'That's enough, Willie,' he said. 'Maybe you're my best
friend, but that's just wicked blasphemy. You've went too
far this time. You're just an old bigot, so you are. I'm
finished wi' ye!'

He emptied his glass and left the bar without another
word, neither hurriedly nor slowly, walking out quite
calmly.

'Christ almighty, some people!' Geddes complained to
the barman. 'Canny take a joke.'

He had another drink to cover his vexation.

'He's no' getting me to go running after him,' he told
the neutral barman. 'Him and his Virgin Mary! I don't
believe a word of it.'

He waited for Rooney to come back and be teased into
conversation again. He waited till the bar closed, and then
he had to plod home alone. Over the next few days he
tried to find Rooney. He went to all the usual places at
the usual times, but he never saw him. His wife, coming
in from her shopping, would tell him she had just seen
Rooney here or there, all by himself, and he acknowledged
the information with a grunt. He didn't want to tell her
Rooney was deliberately avoiding him. He brooded, sour
in his loneliness.

He didn't have to brood long. Rooney died in his sleep
a week later, when a January wind was bringing a sleet
across the village. He was in his chair at the fireside when
his wife bustled in with the news.

'I just met Mrs Lumsden in the grocer's there,' she said.
'She was telling me Liam Rooney passed away during the
night.'

'Och ay,' he nodded with Scottish brevity, showing no
emotion.

He sat forward in his chair, staring into the fire, and as

he looked at the living coals he thought of the pit. Nearly sixty years of working with Rooney jumbled through his mind, and the fire was refracted through his unfallen tears. When he went for his afternoon walk memories of Rooney kept him company. He was passing Sloan's when a young woman crossed the street to speak to him. It was Miss Rooney, teacher of modern languages in the local Catholic secondary school.

'Oh, Willie,' she said, very grave, 'You'll have heard about my father?'

'Oh ay,' he said solemnly, and waited.

'I was on my way round to see you.' Rooney's daughter spoke to him softly. 'My mother sent me. She wants you to take a cord.'

'But that's no' my place, that's for the nearest,' Geddes said, his scalp prickling at the very thought of going to a Catholic funeral. 'And there's all your uncles.'

'Oh, you come before any of them,' she warmed him with a wee smile. 'Some of them have never put a foot across the door for years. You were the first my mother mentioned when she was asked who was all taking a cord.'

'Your mother's very kind,' he said.

He went to see the widow. He guessed at once Rooney had never told her of their last night at the bar. She had no idea her husband's last days on earth were spent avoiding his old butty. He said what he could to show his sympathy, and she gave him hers.

'It was that sudden, Willie,' she whimpered. 'And you'll miss him yourself. After all these years. You and him were through the General Strike thegither and on till that November, and that wasn't yesterday. And he thought the world of you. Every time he came off a shift it was Willie Geddes says this and Willie Geddes says that. Just the night before he died he was talking about you.'

'But how can I go to the funeral?' he asked, screwing

up his eyes. 'Me in a Catholic church! They wouldn't let me in, would they? You know what I am.'

'Now you've no call to be worrying about that,' Mrs Rooney smacked his hand lightly. 'God knows best what we all are. If you think you'd feel strange coming into the church just you meet the party at the door when they bring the body out. All I want you to do is take a cord when they lower the coffin——'

She started to cry again, her own words too blunt for her, and his huge hand patted her shoulder.

'I know Liam would have wanted you there,' she sniffled.

He put on a black tie and his good suit and his dark coat and he went to the funeral. He stood beside the grave while a chubby priest, talking Latin with a Donegal accent, said a lot of prayers he couldn't follow, and when he had taken the cord assigned to him and helped to lower the coffin deep into the damp clay he saw the priest sprinkle water on the lid with a little feather duster. Stuck at the edge of the dismal pit, he felt he was a white man taking part in the rites of a black tribe. On the other side of the grave four of Rooney's unknown brothers, big men with heavy coats and dull faces, huddled together and their lips moved knowingly to the priest's last prayer. When they stopped praying they made the sign of the cross, and determined to be just as much Liam Rooney's mourner as any of them, old Geddes too made the sign of the cross. At that moment he remembered a phrase he had often heard Rooney use, and he repeated it deliberately in a willing suspension of his disbelief.

'God rest him,' he mumbled.

The wind across the cemetery crested his white hair, slapped at the tails of his coat and chilled his old bones.